For Terry —

My very dear
friend for ever!

Love you,

Judy

One Man, Three Taboos

Joy Jones

I am dedicating *One Man, Three Taboos* to Betty Smith of Santa Fe, New Mexico. This friend, a poet and screenwriter herself, encouraged me to begin writing fiction, thus this book.

INFINITY
PUBLISHING.COM

Copyright © 2009 by Joy Jones

ISBN 0-7414-5267-7

Published by:

INFINITY
PUBLISHING.COM

1094 New DeHaven Street, Suite 100
West Conshohocken, PA 19428-2713
Info@buybooksontheweb.com
www.buybooksontheweb.com
Toll-free (877) BUY BOOK
Local Phone (610) 941-9999
Fax (610) 941-9959

Printed in the United States of America

Published April 2009

CHAPTER ONE

She didn't have time to listen, but his eyes wouldn't let her get on with her usual Thursday. The hall in the Educational Center for Excellence at Northern Arizona University that spring morning was crowded with students and faculty, and it had seemed harmless enough to speak to the man whose face she remembered from one of her grad classes last semester. However, she hadn't anticipated his hunger to be acknowledged, so now she found herself impatient and stuck in an imminent conversation that held little interest for her.

"How have you been?" he asked tentatively. "I haven't seen you in class this semester." Leisa Jennings recognized a foreign accent, but the way he was soaking up her appearance got more of her attention. He made no attempt to camouflage his approval of her tall, svelte body; her smiling face (could he see that it wasn't genuine?), and her casual, Norwegian-blond hair.

She answered hurriedly, "Oh, going crazy as usual. Between the six hours of classes I'm taking this semester, and my job here as student teacher coordinator, I don't even have the energy to go dancing. And THAT is not my idea of living." Her breathless manner was a clue that she wasn't prepared to stop and chat, but the man didn't get it.

"You are so very beautiful," was his off the subject response to her small talk. "It is a pleasure to be in your company." How did he manage to mix familiarity with an appropriate air of reserve, she wondered.

"Thank you", spoken quickly and without any relish, preceded the only comment she could think of, in an effort to make their exchange less personal. "I think that I remember that you will be finished with your studies here this spring, won't you?"

"Oh, for sure, I will be returning to my country, Burkina Faso in Africa after graduation. It has been a long two years here." He smiled, but his large, ebony eyes were lifeless. His English was perfect, flavored with a foreign accent, but spiritless.

She kept standing there. She couldn't walk away. Minutes of casual conversation were eating up her work day, but she couldn't leave the black man who held her with melancholy eyes. She had to get back to her office so she was surprised, and certainly perplexed, to hear herself invite him to go with her.

Leisa's office was the only one she had ever had. Being a school teacher from Texas, this having an office and a secretary was a new experience for her. Actually the word 'new' as applied to her life about covered it. When she left Texas three years ago in search of her next life, she was confident of only one thing – she did not want to spend another year in a classroom with teenagers. Therefore, since her only work experience was in education, she felt blessed to get the Student Teacher Coordinator position there at NAU. The only drawback with it was that the salary was so

2

meager that she could barely make ends meet. However, it didn't cost much to go dancing at the Zoo, a historic saloon and dance hall, there in Flagstaff. It was famous for having tall tree trunks going up through the dance floor, reaching to the rafters that were loaded with preserved and mounted animals. There was never any lack of cowboys to dance with, and since Leisa was not in the market for romance, she attracted them like flies. Yes, her life was most enjoyable when not complicated with a relationship. Her long marriage to a Texas rancher had produced two children and she now had two precious, baby granddaughters. Needless to say, the last thing on her list was another marriage. Therefore, she limited her social life to dancing at the Zoo every Friday night, dinner parties with girl friends on Saturdays, and her own company during the work week.

He took the chair across from the desk, thus her afternoon work plan was put on hold. His body language told her that he was overwhelmed with emotion as his words told her about his life as a student at NAU. Could it be possible that his tale was true? This man was a thirty year old international student, a Fullbright scholar, a guest in her country, living in a dorm with an eighteen year old roommate. Yet, for two years, this visitor from Africa had never been any farther off campus than a distance he was willing to walk. No professor or student had invited him into their home. Consequently, his experience of the United States had been courtesy of the TV and classmates at a university who had been cordial to him, but ignored him as a human being. And, she realized, she had to be included in that number. Yes, now that she thought about it, she could remember seeing him in her classes, but she had never even considered talking to him. And evidently, everyone else looked right past him too. Not with intended hurt, but it had.

As time ticked by unnoticed, she listened to his story, and wondered how she could have been so completely unaware of this fascinating man. Those soulful eyes, framed by perfectly sculpted thick eyebrows, competed with his generous mouth and gleaming white teeth for her attention. Undeniably, in any color – black, white, red, brown, or yellow – he would be judged a handsome man. His wide, high forehead was edged with hair cut so short as to render it unnecessary. The flawless face was hairless and his high cheekbones could have been courtesy of a Cherokee Indian heritage like hers. Yes, his story was pitiful, but he was not. Regal he was. Sitting there erect, yet unassuming. The ringing phone didn't even distract her from this compelling man in her office. She said very little. He talked and talked, yet she intuitively knew that his mind was more on her, than on his story. Therefore, when a rare smile did come to his impressive face, his eyes began to reflect an unfamiliar feel, and his new-found desire to smile was like a magnet to her soul.

"I will be going back to my family, my wife and daughter, who live in Ouagadougou. That is the capitol city of Burkina Faso. Upon my return, I will take a teaching post at the university. It is like this, my destiny was determined when I was only a child. You see, I am to serve my people by helping them to advance in education, and too, I have a financial responsibility to my parents and siblings." He spoke with such authority that it didn't register with Leisa to

4

question his philosophy of 'destiny'.

Long before he ended his story, her 'fix it NOW' habit to any problem, (whether it was hers or not), kicked in. She started thinking of how she might remedy a situation that embarrassed her as an American and a human being. For instance, she could invite him to join her circle of friends for dancing, the movies, or one of their Saturday night pot luck dinners. So as he was leaving, she encouraged him with the promise that she would be calling him with a social invitation of some sort. However, her concentration on ways to improve his life were sabotaged when he took her shoulders firmly in his hands, and quickly touched his cheek to each of hers, as he thanked her for the visit.

She wasn't ignorant of the gesture. She had seen it many times in movies as a welcome or a farewell, but it was the effect of his energy, when their bodies were momentarily close, that had her mystified. How very strange, she thought, as she sat down at her desk to get busy with neglected work. Knowing that nothing is by chance, as the rest of the afternoon passed, she pondered this unusual and initially unwelcomed interlude.

"Leisa? Is this Leisa Jennings?"

"Yes," she answered into the telephone. It was five o'clock and she was exhausted from an afternoon of effort to focus on her job.

"This is Yaro Bomou. Please, I just wanted to express to you how gracious was your company today, and I am calling to thank you for the conversation."

Warmth and compassion washed over her, and she said with heart felt genuineness, "You are very welcome."

And then, adding quickly before she dared to let herself think about it, "I haven't had time to contact anyone else, but if you would like to join me, I'm going hiking this Sunday in Sedona, and I was thinking that you might enjoy seeing that beautiful part of our state. It is less than an hour's drive from here down the switch-backs."

His response was immediate, passionate and affirmative. She would pick him up at his dorm late Sunday morning. The phone fell lifeless from her hand, and instead of leaving her office she turned off the light and sank into a chair near the large picture window to watch the last snow fall that always came in March. As she watched the tree limbs sway, accusing questions in her mind demanded answers.

'What in the shit are you doing? What? What? Oh, sure, it's the good Samaritan thing, right? And you want me to believe that you aren't in the least bit attracted to him, right? Oh really? Okay, okay...unwarranted hysteria from the good sense department of your brain. I am to disregard the fact that you are a forty two year old single woman with no intention of getting romantically involved with anyone? And this isn't a problem? A man who is the victim of desperate loneliness and not just any man, but a black, married man who is probably younger too! So sure, there's absolutely nothing wrong with this picture. Good lord, Leisa!! You make me crazy!

Her heart and her mind waged constant battle as the days marched toward Sunday. What was she doing? Why would she risk getting involved with this inappropriate man? Improper, immoral, and no-future is the definition of 'inappropriate' in this instance. According to his university records, he was twelve years younger and yes, married. Certainly it was crystal clear that their involvement could create negative, life altering consequences for them both.

As she sat at her desk watching the oak tree resist the strong March wind (instead of preparing the workshop for the student teacher supervisors), she allowed her mind to wander back to her life in Texas. It had been almost five years since she had divorced the father of her children, and even though she did not regret leaving a man whose only crime was that he bored her to death, she could still, at times, disregard what all the self-help books say, and feel guilty about it. Happily, all was friendly now because she and her ex-husband got along beautifully; there was no evidence that their children were damaged by the divorce, and the rural southern town had finally taken her out of its 'wicked-woman' box, and instead, now days, labeled her that 'unorthodox Auntie Mame' type instead. Actually, it was sort of fun to answer the first question hometown folks always asked, "And where are you now?"

Was it only yesterday at the department luncheon meeting that she had entertained the ladies with her views about intimate relationships? Having all women for an audience, she had assured them that if a woman-over-forty was healthy, financially secure, and had a passionate interest in either her work or hobby, then a man was only icing. Not necessary, but perfect for adding flavor to her already happy, life cake. Now, here it was a day later and she was struggling with her attraction to a man who would not qualify as 'icing'. Maybe this is what single women do. They maintain a party line of, 'men are not necessary for happiness', yet lurking underneath this glib exterior of exuberance lurks a willingness to risk disaster for a romantic possibility.

"It's been a long dry spell, hasn't it Leisa?" she said aloud to the empty office. "Maybe that has something to do with me even entertaining the idea of this man." Talking to herself had been a life-long habit.

He was waiting for her Sunday outside the dorm. As he sat down in the front seat of Shotsy, her red Honda Civic, his presence overwhelmed the small interior. Yaro was a tall man with a body that appeared to be one well-toned muscle. But it was the blackness of his being that filled Shotsy's space. However, there was no threat in his nearness or even any sexual overtones to his demeanor. With an unfamiliar twinge of something, she realized, it had to be his blackness that was the reason for her discomfort. But, how could that be, she wondered, as she greeted the smiling man beside her, and headed Shotsy toward the switchbacks to Sedona.

Having been born and raised in the south, Leisa was not a stranger to the black race. In fact, a most cherished childhood friend had been a Negro boy who had worked on her dad's dairy farm. Being the same age and size, they had shared everything from riding the one old horse across the pasture to head the cows to the barn; to lunch and a matinee movie on Saturdays (after being scrubbed clean of the morning's dirt by her mother), and to even the whipping they would both get after every trip home, down the railroad tracks from town. It was the same story every Saturday. The movie manager would catch her sitting upstairs in the 'colored' balcony with Henry; call her mom, and that would get them the belt as the finale of the day. Years later, she had questioned her mother about this weekly ritual.

She had said, "There was nothing wrong with Henry. He was your friend and you could play all you wanted to here at home. However, when you go to town, that's different." Of course, that was not an explanation, but even so, Leisa was sure that even now her mother would say the same thing. How was it possible to hand down prejudice to a child without being aware of it in yourself?

Leisa was positive that she had never felt prejudice against any race. Just last summer, she had been a roommate to her black co-worker. Yet, she had to acknowledge, in the same breath, that she had never before now been physically attracted to a man of another race. So, how could she know, until now, that any chemistry between the races she would experience as forbidden? Did no conscious awareness on her part excuse this reality? Thank goodness Yaro's comfortable, easy conversation forced her mind away from her uncomfortable soul searching.

He was so hungry to talk. As she drove slowly down the switchbacks, she answered his questions about the country he had lived in for the past two years....yet had experienced so little of, punctuated with gasps of wonder for nature's spectacular red rock mountains, and the fast running creek bordered by densely wooded banks.

Leisa shared nothing about herself. Yaro Bomou was starved for an audience, and that's the role she chose for this Sunday drama. She drove, listened, answered questions about Sedona and the western United States and delighted in his company. Actually, she felt like Santa Claus! Everything was such a thrill for him, even choosing what to order at Arby's. He thanked her over and over for treating him to a picnic lunch.

"I want you to experience Bell Rock, so let's have our lunch there," Leisa explained as she drove out of Arby's parking lot to take the road towards the Village of Oak Creek. The sun was high, and the always-perfect blue sky was brilliant. Yaro was enraptured by everything: the red rocks, the friendly people on the trail up Bell Rock Mountain, and her guiding presence. But as they sat down under the shade of a fat, high-desert tree, their togetherness took center stage.

"Aren't you hungry?" Leisa asked.

"Oh, for sure", he answered quickly. But she saw in his eyes what he didn't say... "but for more than this sandwich".

With those unspoken words, the casual day was gone. His eyes were large, luminous, sable pools of emotion. None of her attempts at naming the distant hills, the variety of vegetation, or pointing out the different blues in the sky had succeeded in directing his eyes from her. All her ownership of wrong-doing was back in that moment. She realized immediately that her earlier relief that the day would be spent in a casual, unemotional way was foolish. There was no way that this man could be experienced airily. His very presence completely captured her senses. She was in the wrong place, doing the wrong thing, with the wrong man!

She could no longer doubt her bigotry. Prejudice!

She couldn't even think the word, but she could feel it. All day, whenever they weren't alone: ordering food in Arby's, and then walking up the trail in the presence of other people, she was aware of being stiff and ill-at-ease. This robbed her of the enjoyment that should have been her experience. Because she assumed that all those strangers saw them as a couple, a cold, hard knot formed in her stomach, and the wave of unwanted thoughts caused a flood of emotions that left her reeling with proof positive of a warp in her soul.

Not so for Yaro. He enjoyed having the other hikers interrupt them with questions, and he showed no sign of realizing her discomfort. It took him a long time to finish his lunch. And, even though she knew he must be enjoying eating something other than dorm food, she felt that his complete attention was on her. Her attempts at light chatter were met with only perfunctory interest, and the man who had talked constantly in her car, was now silent. His manner was not intrusive, but the sadness and longing in those eyes made guilt bubble up from her upset stomach and finally silence her. There was no more talking. She couldn't look at him so she just sat there, hugging her knees to her chest, and fixing her gaze on a distant point.

Moments passed, but eventually, judging from the noise of the paper bag, he had finished eating. Only when he called her name did she look at him. "Leisa, I have something to give you." He said in a hushed voice that was fractured with emotion. She turned to see him pulling a small bunch of plastic flowers and an envelope out of one of the two white grocery bags he had brought with him.

"Please, is it okay? I want to present a gift for your

kindness, but I don't know about these things in your country. And please, this letter is for you."

She accepted the fake flowers he had walked to K-Mart to buy with more sensation than she ever had had with expensive roses, and as she took the envelope from this man's trembling hand, she felt somehow trapped in her own power. Without meeting his eyes, she mumbled assurances that the flowers were perfect, and she opened the letter to read silently.

"Dear Leisa,

Thank you so much for your special concern and deep empathy toward me, through the hard times I am living due to moral hardships, and psychological and emotional breakdown. I cannot fully express my gratitude and appreciation for this highly kind act. I am overwhelmed. Your generous comfort that you freely award me, allows me to hope for the best during the rest of my stay at the university. This is a wonderful blessing for me; a generosity that touches my heart. You make me very happy, for you are helping me get out of these deadly blues and see a flicker of hope, joy and emotional brightness. You are a kind and noble person because you are truthfully endowed with a humane heart. I will hold a special place in my heart for you and I shall always call you my friend. Please accept my humble thanks, full of the kindness and caring you have shown me, as well as these flowers that symbolize your awesome feminine beauty, tripled with your dazzling charm and your indescribable elegance.

Yaro Bomou"

She couldn't breathe. Instantaneously, it registered with her that he hadn't learned the red-blooded, All-American man's way of expressing himself. No, he exposed himself completely as her admirer. That certainly was not the way to play the dating game. But her next thought focused on herself. She was as fake as the artificial flowers in her lap. Fake! He was not the wrong man! She was the wrong woman!

Leisa responded with an automatic, "What a wonderful compliment. Thank you." She could only look at him fleetingly as she gathered up their things and suggested they continue their hike. Her glance at his face revealed his mixture of worry, hope, and uncertainty. Her thoughts were a mixture of dismay and ambiguity. She was incredibly attracted to this man, yet the reality that he was black outdistanced the fact that he was married and so much younger. Where was she during the 1960's when soul searching for hidden prejudice was in style? How could she be having this experience three decades later? But for now, all she could do was lead the way, so they moved up the trail in silence.

Their footsteps made the only sounds as they hiked Indian style up the mountain because there weren't other people around them now. Obviously he was behind her, and following her lead, but neither of them made any attempt at conversation.

"I'm going to leave you here," she said, as she motioned to a huge rock right off the path.

"It is my habit to do my TM at about this time of day.

I'll just be up there a little ways for about thirty minutes. Will that be okay?"

"Oh, this is good, Leisa. It is time for my prayers," he said as he held up the other plastic bag she had wondered about. "I have my prayer rug and beads. So I will wait here for you."

She was so full of her own concerns that for once she didn't even notice if her uncomfortable quick glance was perceived as anything other than her usual 'everything is just fine' look. She wanted to run away and leave him there forever. Instead, she found a private spot that was out of his sight, and sat down to escape into her meditation. Her deep breaths would quiet her pounding heart and her mantra would take her away, away from the circumstances of this Sunday afternoon. Being a long time meditator, she seldom had trouble going within, but today she got no such reprieve. The tape entitled, "No, No, No! Not This Man Now, Or Ever", sabatoged her meditation attempts, thus she didn't return to Yaro Bomou with the peace she needed.

Where had all the people gone? The mountain was silent and lonely. She could see Yaro standing near a large rock with his back to her. His body was rigid and he was unaware of her return, so she announced her presence by calling his name. He turned slowly and his eyes held hers for one short second before he dropped to the ground on his knees.

Leisa felt, as well as saw, his despair, and at that moment her instinct as a mother kicked in. Had he not stopped her with a wave of his hand, she would have taken him into her arms to offer comfort, solace, help….whatever he needed for his pain.

"No, Leisa. Do not touch me." His voice was commanding, but the eyes that looked up at her were tender. "I can't guarantee my behavior if you touch me. Only sit with me here, please."

As Leisa sat down beside him, he remained on his knees. Silence reigned between them for several minutes. Her initial concern for Yaro gave way to her own mounting emotion of helplessness for herself, as well as him. She was so engulfed by her own feelings, that for a second, she didn't realize he was finally talking to her.

"....I am traveling through the ages and to a foreign space. The karma between us is a vortex that has been whirling my heart in your direction all my life. Allah's plan, not my own, because nothing fits our reality. I am a man from a foreign culture with not so many years on this earth as you, and I am already married. Nevertheless Leisa, I am connected to you. Destiny will bring us together in Allah's time."

There was nothing for her to say, even had she known how to respond. As the gathering twilight spread its evening shadows over them, Leisa was under attack by her thoughts. A black, married, younger man! And was it possible that her paramount concern was his race? Why didn't the fact that he was married at least worry her as much? And his being twelve years younger didn't fit with the rules either. Man's restrictive rules! An anger sprinkled with fear rose in her chest. She had never realized until this moment what an unquestioned hold society's precepts had on her. It made her feel owned and controlled. Too, unlike

15

Yaro, she didn't have any religious belief to give her faith in some Divine plan for their lives. All she felt was despair as she stood up and signaled for him to do the same. Their descent down the trail was a silent one. Once in her car, the only thing she could think of to say was, "Do you like ice cream? Let's stop somewhere on the way back and get some."

CHAPTER TWO

It was like Sunday had never happened. Yaro either called or came by her office every day the following week, but neither of them made any reference to their Sunday together in Sedona. He would say only a brief, casual thing or two, but his smile was equivalent to a deep gentleness, a full, immovable acceptance of their togetherness. So, as it happened, their unspoken agreement to not acknowledge the unwanted ingredients of their relationship reality culminated in a Saturday night invitation to dinner at her house. Leisa told herself it would be an opportunity for Yaro to enjoy the company of her roommate Jon and a friend of his from Sedona. Too, there would be no opportunity for the temptation for physical intimacy between them. So, armed with this protection from herself, she made plans for an informal meal of Louisiana stew and cornbread.

She had to go to her office on Saturday morning to catch up on paper work, and was stressed to find herself driving the 17 miles into Flagstaff in a storm. Snow again! Would the winter ever be over? Safe in her office, however, she could enjoy the beauty of the snow-covered tree outside her window, but driving in it was scary. Safely there now, and with no one around to talk to, she was sure to finish all she needed to do and even more. Being an over-achiever had its rewards. She was actually happy to be working away on a Saturday morning for no extra pay.

She hadn't expected the phone to ring. It was her housemate Jon, with the news that his date couldn't come, and that he would be driving instead to Sedona for the weekend. "You can't! I don't care how she feels about driving in the snow. You promised me."

"I'm really sorry, Leisa," Jon apologized. "But you know how she is. There is nothing I can do."

Oh God! No, no, no! Now she would have to break her dinner date with Yaro. With the weather the way it was, it was obvious that he would have to be staying over. No one, not even the skilled local drivers, would venture out tonight. But, without her roommate and his date in attendance, there was no way. She could not; would not, be alone with Yaro in her home. But, how in the world was she going to break the date? Immediately, the 'why' took the place of the 'how'. Was this the Universe's way of stopping this relationship before it went any further? Or, was it the opposite…the way made possible for what Yaro called karma between them?

Within minutes, he entered Leisa's office, right on time, carrying a plastic grocery bag. She knew by now that it contained his Moslem prayer paraphernalia. His eyes were shining and his face aglow. She couldn't hesitate. She had to immediately explain how the weather was responsible for the cancellation of their plans.

"We will just postpone our dinner together until next weekend," she finished lamely. He sat in the chair across from her desk and said nothing. There were no tears or any sign of being shattered by her lament. Silence reigned for what felt like an eternity. When he did speak, his voice was calm and heavy.

"I am not a child, Leisa. You have decided not to take me to your house because of the taboos…a married man, a younger man, and a very, very black man."

As she sat frozen in front of him, she struggled with how to claim something about herself that she had never known before, prejudice. God, what an awful word. Sure he was twelve years younger, and married, but those two details weren't causing her the anguish they should. He wasn't white! That was it. Finally he continued in a manner that was both regal and burdened. "Please Leisa; don't do this thing to me. I will die. If you send me back to that dorm, I will die."

Because of the snow storm, her total attention had to be focused on the highway. Yaro was silent, but not in a sullen way. He was intent on the beautiful white world; almost no people, and slow moving cars. However, time didn't need any words. She sensed that he was not upset by their conversation in her office; that he had moved on in his mind to embrace only this moment. She couldn't. Her eyes were on the road and her hands gripped the steering wheel tightly, but her ego was in full control of her mind. As she inched Shotsy toward home, it was like watching herself in a drama that she couldn't leave. She didn't have a leg to stand on. How could she defend herself when his charge was true, and she knew he knew it was. Hurt! This whole relationship was covered in hurt. The only question was… now, or later? As the garage door opened to let them into the safe, warm house, she knew that the answer was 'later'.

She loved her home in the woods in the small village of Munds Park. It was a rental only until the summer, but she and Jon had furnished it comfortably. They both had their own bedroom and bath; the kitchen window provided a view of the local elk wandering through the yard in the early morning, and the fireplace in the living room drew everyone near. Today, the aroma of Louisiana stew in the crock pot welcomed the unlikely pair.

Yaro followed her into the house and stood transfixed before Jon's tall grandfather clock in the living room. His total interest was on her home, and she knew to leave him to explore it. As he moved from room to room, he would occasionally call a question that she answered from the kitchen. It occurred to her that his attention to the contents of the house was the perfect opening for the conversation she was now ready to have. So when she had finished with the dinner preparations, she directed him to the seating area in front of the blazing fireplace and announced, "It is time for you to tell me about you and your world. I know nothing about the country, Burkina Faso. Start there," she instructed as she turned off the tape in her head. With her legs hugging her chest, and a glass of Pinot Griego in her hand (no wine for him, of course..... being Moslem, it was forbidden), she was ready to listen.

He rearranged his body in the big, comfortable chair closest to the couch as he said, "Of course. Yes. Well, it is a very poor, landlocked country located in the middle of West Africa's 'hump'. I would say that the average yearly income would be less than 500 dollars. The mining of limited

20

amounts of manganese, gold, and marble is our major industry, other than agriculture. The sixty three different ethnic groups in Burkina Faso are integrated in a secular state that has been independent since 1960. Life there is very hard, Leisa. Not like here in your country. People don't often live past 50 years, and the literacy rate is only 26%. That is why I am here. It is my life's purpose to improve the educational level of my people."

"So it is your destiny to be here? To get your masters degree? To return to your country to work there as an educator?"

"For sure. It is set for me. I will go home in May to teach at the university there in Ouagadougou. My students will be preparing to teach in our country, and it will be my job to acquaint them with the curriculum I have learned here at NAU. Then I will be back."

"You will? When? Why?" She was sure he heard the anticipation in her voice.

"To get my doctorate in educational leadership. That degree will make it possible for me to be accepted by the Ministry of Education, and work for the progress needed in my country. I will be traveling to schools in all the major towns in Burkina Faso to help advance them into the 21st century. For sure, it is my destiny."

There was such assurance in his manner. Her eyes traveled over his body as he got up from his chair to put another log on the fire. For a man from such humble circumstances, he exuded a royal demeanor. Was that what a sense of destiny gave a person, she wondered. "Tell me more about this destiny thing. I don't have a sense of it myself, but judging from what the history books say about Napoleon, he believed that destiny directed his life from a young age."

"Well," began Yaro, "destiny refers to a predetermined course of events. It can be seen as a fixed sequence of events that is inevitable and unchangeable, or that individuals choose their own destiny by choosing different paths throughout their life."

"Okay – then, I have two questions for you. Do you choose your path or is it unchangeable? And, what is the difference between fate and destiny? I find it all confusing," admitted Leisa.

Yaro smiled as he continued, "Although the words are used interchangeably in many cases, fate and destiny can be distinguished. Fate is a power that predetermines and orders the course of events. Fate defines events as 'meant to be'. Fate is used in regard to the finality of events as they have worked themselves out. Fate implies no choice.....and many times ends with a death. Fate is determined by something outside the person that is acting upon the person. However, with destiny the person is participating in achieving an outcome that is directly related to him or her. Participation happens willfully. For example, my parents chose me to be educated, but if I had failed in school or not accepted my responsibility to help my family by becoming educated, then I would have denied my destiny."

Leisa was puzzled, "I'm sorry but I don't entirely get it. On the one hand, you weren't in control because your parents chose you. Yet, on the other hand, you were in control because you studied and succeeded. So where exactly does the concept fit into that scenario?"

Yaro was silent for a minute and she could tell that he was trying to put what he so strongly believed into words she could understand. Finally he said, "Destiny is a concept based on the belief that there is a fixed order to the universe. This plan for our lives is in place at birth. However, all people have the free will to accept it or reject it. I am sure you have heard it said, 'he fulfilled his destiny', or 'he fell short of his destiny'. Some of it is meant-to-be, and some of it is believing in it, and then working hard to achieve it. Leisa, I guess it is just something one knows without proof."

"That makes sense. Yeah, I think I can understand. If I limited what I believed by what could be proved, I'd be minus lots of concepts I experience as the truth. So, yes…. I can accept that".

"I was the one of twelve children chosen by my parents to be educated. I call that destiny because it completely changed my life. Too, even as a young child I felt the responsibility of it because I was to be my family's way out of poverty. And even though it took me away from my parents and all my brothers and sisters for the rest of my life, I was inspired to do my best."

"Where was your home in Burkina Faso, and why did you have to leave it to become educated?" interrupted Leisa.

"You cannot imagine my home. It is a very small village along the Mouhoun River that flows through a savanna plateau of fields, brush, and scattered trees. Only small craft can navigate it. And it is a shame that the infrastructure is not in place for tourism because my country has the largest elephant population in West Africa. Too, we

23

have lions, hippos, monkeys, warthogs, and antelope."

"So your parents had to send you away to go to school?"

"But, of course. Leisa, there were no schools in the village. At the age of seven I began my fourteen years of boarding schools and college dorm life. My parents and siblings worked to pay for my education. So when I completed my education at the university in Ouagadougou, the capitol of Burkina Faso, I started my teaching career there in that city."

"Then, you have never been back to your village to live? You have lived most of your life away from your family? Do you feel like you even know any of those people? Surely that must feel like a sacrifice."

"Not at all. I love my family very much, but we are not personal. They sacrificed for me, so I readily sacrifice for them now and in the future. I will always send money back to my family in the village of my youth."

"But evidently you wanted more education."

"Oh, for sure. That is why I studied day and night to win the Fullbright Scholarship to come to your country to earn my masters degree. If I am to advance to a position of educational influence, I must have degrees from countries other than Burkina Faso. That is why I hope to be back to get my doctorate here in the United States or possibly France. It is my destiny to earn a PhD." His eyes told her that she too was now part of his destiny, and that communication gave her the opening she needed to ask about his wife.

"Okay, Yaro. Now you must tell me about your wife. And, do you have children?" For a second she let her thoughts wander away from his story, and was perplexed to notice that she felt little distress around the fact that he was married.

"Ah yes, Anzounou. My wife's name is Anzounou, and she too is a teacher. That is how we met. We were both teachers for four years at the same school in Ouagadougou. She understands and honors my destiny, so after we were married she helped me for five years to study and prepare for the day I would leave her and our one daughter to come to America."

She had to ask. There was no point in avoiding the obvious. Clearly, he was as attracted to her as she was to him, despite the fact that there had been no physical contact between them, and more importantly, last Sunday he had proclaimed to her that she was his destiny.

"So how do you deal with today…..this minute? You are alone with me in my home. You have told me that you feel this mysterious and incredible connection to me. You call it destiny. Yet, you are married. And, you are leaving in a few weeks to go almost around the globe from me. How does this work? We aren't talking generalities here. This is you and me in a life that does not fit with what you feel is your destiny. "For God's sake," Leisa finished with an exasperated rush of words rising an octave higher, "you won't even touch me."

Yaro sat motionless. She could see the passionate desire in his eyes. The fire crackled, the wind blew against the window, and the sun was now long gone. She sipped her wine as she turned away from his eyes to stare at the fire. She knew that his eyes were on her. She felt the connection.

There was no meaning to it, just a nameless recognition that consumed her. She took a deep breath and waited for him to speak.

"Ah, Leisa. None of your culture's social bans has anything to do with it, and the circumstances of my life today….this minute….alone with you here in your home are not to be questioned. You are part of my destiny and I have known this since last Sunday when you left me there on Bell Rock to pray. We are only to trust it. Can you do that?"

"But you are married," she cried…hating the way she sounded so desperate.

"And that is why I haven't touched you and won't. The only way I can maintain restraint and honor my wife is to not physically caress you. I must rely on you feeling the love I have for you despite no physical, and certainly, no sexual contact."

She didn't answer. Instead, she probed her thoughts anew. Somehow it was softening to sense that she needed to follow his advice and remove the trauma from the drama she was living. Could she let go of all the judgments she automatically placed on the people and events of her life? Could she accept this evening and this man as a blessing, instead of a lapse into immorality? Yes, as something wrapped in mystery that was not a problem at all, but a gift from the Universe?

It was clear that he didn't need an answer. Could he read her mind, as she suspected? The energy between them shifted and an air of casualness and familiarity carried them through dinner. Her cornbread was his favorite dish, and she wasn't surprised. Her mother's recipe was her claim to fame, and Leisa loved serving it. She had to restrict herself to making it only for company, because she had been known to sit down and eat the a whole pan by herself. Talk and dinner ended and together they returned to the living room and the cozy fire that was waiting for them. No music or conversation were needed. Each sat in their own space, yet Leisa couldn't ever remember feeling more joined in heart and spirit with another human being. Eventually she left him to his night's rest on the couch with only the company of Jon's grandfather clock.

* * * * *

Spring seemed to arrive overnight, and suddenly Leisa's life was on fast forward. She and Yaro would eat lunch together two or three times a week (Leisa treating him to a variety of cafes off campus), and they spent some portion of every weekend together. Arizona was the perfect state for spectacular variety in nature, and after much thought she decided that the Grand Canyon was to follow Sedona as the next place to experience with Yaro. She had been there once years earlier, but it was just a short visit on the South Rim during a return trip from Las Vegas. Needless to say, she didn't know any of the history or culture of the canyon, and she was sorry she hadn't read up on it before telling Yaro that she was planning a day hike on the South Rim. His enthusiasm she enjoyed but lord, all those questions she couldn't answer! Thank goodness the Chamber of Commerce there in Flagstaff had tons of material for him to pour over, so by the time the weekend rolled around, *he* educated *her* as she drove them towards

Grand Canyon Village.

"Diarabi, let me tell you about the split-twig figurines." This African term of endearment was the only name he ever used for her now. "According to all I have read this week about the archeology of the canyon, they are some of the oldest and most fascinating artifacts found there. Each one is made from a single twig, often willow, split down the middle, and then carefully folded into animal shapes. These figurines date from 2,000 to 4,000 years ago and were often found in remote caves. They are in the shape of deer or bighorn sheep, sometimes with horns or antlers. Occasionally, they are pierced with another stick, resembling a spear, or are stuffed with artiodactyls dung. While their exact function remains a mystery, recent research suggest that split-twig figurines were totems associated with the late archaic hunting and gathering culture. Their occurrence in remote, relatively inaccessible uninhabited caves indicates that these figurines were not toys. They are usually found under rock cairns, indicating careful placement. It says here that these amazing and ancient figurines can be viewed at the Tusayan Museum. Do you think we will have time to visit the museum?"

"I don't see why not," Leisa smiled affirmatively. She loved his interest in every thing, and his appetite for the unknown was amazing. No wonder he had been a successful student for most of his life. She continued, "The only thing we have planned to do is take a day hike and the one I think would be most suited to our time and interests is the Rim Trail. There are some really steep, physically demanding hikes, but I'm not up for that. Do you agree?"

"For sure, I want to have the time and energy to visit the village area, but also experience walking along the rim. It says here in this brochure that the Rim Trail extends from the village area to Hermits Rest. It offers excellent walking and quiet views of the inner canyon for visitors who desire an easy hike. Is that us?" he laughed.

There it was again, Leisa realized, as she stood next to the rail looking out to the majestic world of the Grand Canyon. Yaro was standing next to her and she wasn't easy and relaxed with that because of the other tourists standing near or walking by. She still found herself wondering how they felt about her being with a black man. Damn it to hell!!! What would it take for this sense of wrong-doing to go away? There was no rational reason for it. In no way did she feel superior to him. What a laugh that was. Actually, if there were a contest, he would be judged superior to her. No doubt his IQ was off the charts, and how many languages could he speak as compared to her one? It had to be cultural, she concluded, as she once again forced it out of her mind.

Leisa waited until mid-May, so the water would be as warm as possible, to plan their weekend trip to Lake Powell. She had been there several times with friends who had a houseboat, and it was one of her all-time favorite places in the world. Cruising on clear blue waters beneath high red rock cliff walls, bathed in warm sunshine, was something she wanted Yaro to experience. Her preference would have been to explore serpentine finger canyons and swim together, but since neither she nor Yaro would be able to manage driving a houseboat, she instead wrangled an invitation for them to be guests of her friends.

The plan was for Leisa and Yaro to meet them at Wahweap Marina, the largest and most popular access point at the southwestern end of the lake. There were two reasons for this: one – she was certain Yaro would want to tour the Glen Canyon Dam that had created the lake, and secondly – she wanted to be alone with him for the drive from Flagstaff to Page, AZ. The two couples were relatively new and casual friends and to be perfectly honest, it was the opportunity to enjoy Lake Powell on a houseboat that kept them in Leisa's life. They were retired military and their idea of a perfect evening was to start with cocktails at 5 pm; repeat their stories of life on foreign posts ad-nausea; eat a wonderful meal under the stars, and then fall into bed and be asleep by 9 pm. They would get up around noon and spend the afternoon catching the plentiful fish in the crystalline water, then repeat the previous evening's drinking, stories, and dining. Since Yaro didn't drink and he was more of an intellect than all four of them put together, she was a little uncertain about how the socializing would go.

He certainly knew how to be attentive to their conversation, Leisa thought, as she sat back to watch the interaction between Yaro and her friends. It didn't take long for him to realize that they weren't much interested in his life or country, so he easily moved into the position of being a new listener for theirs. Over cocktails and dinner he was very personable and a good audience for their many tales. Actually, he was probably not faking it at all. His appetite for new people and topics carried him through the Saturday night party without a hitch. Leisa was the one having some trouble. Not with any one of her friends or Yaro, but with herself - and more specifically - with her thoughts. What must they think of her, she wondered, as she remained outside the conversation yet in the social circle? These two couples had been married forever, and they had lived their lives by the unyielding military code of right and wrong. Therefore, Leisa had known not to tell them that Yaro was married, even though they presented themselves as just friends. She didn't want them to think less of her or Yaro either, for that matter. Leisa was hoping that her request for separate sleeping arrangements would take care of any social impropriety.

What she realized, she noted, as her analyze-it-to-death habit took over her mind, surprised her. Of the three no-no's, his being married bothered her least. Why was that, she pondered, as she smiled; sipped her scotch and soda, and faked an interest in the conversation she wasn't a part of. Two possibilities occurred to her. Was it because, having been divorced, she didn't really honor the popular notion of marriage being a forever thing, once you signed up? And, would that translate into the possibility that Yaro just might get a divorce too? Leisa couldn't see that happening, so her philosophical concept about the role of marriage must be it. She had often toyed with the notion that marriage really served only one good purpose in these modern times, and that was to have children. Marriage is a necessary part of life, but because time changes people, it just lasts too long. Maybe the arrangement should be that you can re-enlist if things are good, but end it without all the trauma/drama of divorce, if it is over. "Or maybe, oh cynical one, you just haven't had the right man yet. Maybe you would die to be

31

married to Yaro as decades moved towards old age," she muttered to herself as she made her way to the boat's bar for another scotch.

Two weeks later a Saturday party with her two friends from Albuquerque, New Mexico and Phoenix, Arizona was the perfect opportunity to enjoy Yaro in a social setting of predominately women: a red-head with natural curly hair that framed a nymph-like face; a brunette with long hair and an air of city sophistication that even her ponytail and jeans couldn't mask, and the blond who could have been Leisa's twin with those large, bold, blue eyes that had taken many a prisoner. Jon's lady friend from Sedona (the red-head) was really attracted to Yaro. As he filled the afternoon hours with stories of his country, Jon's girlfriend became more and more certain that she had lived a past life in Africa (Leisa suspected that the wine had much to do with her certainty).

Yaro's story of his childhood was right out of some novel about mysterious, dark Africa. He began simply with, "I was raised in a mud house with a thatched roof. During vacation time away from my boarding school, I herded our cows in the bush all day long from early morning until sunset. Like me, the villagers too worked hard, but there was little to show for our labors." As he talked on, Leisa found it almost impossible to envision him in the primitive world he described.

The video of his family's village that he had taken before he left home added to everyone's understanding. The film was like a documentary in that it showed the trip up the river to his village and the home of his parents. They were

32

such happy people in very simple surroundings. Anzounou, his wife, was radiantly beautiful in brilliantly colored native dress, and she was clearly the center of attention. Leisa wasn't surprised that Anzounou was elegant and sophisticated. Any wife of Yaro's would be. She moved like a queen in every scene she was in; she didn't wave or smile like a child for the camera, yet her black eyes were warm and welcoming.

The family home was a compound of two small buildings, with a dining table and chairs under a shady tree in a fenced yard of packed, swept earth. Small children were playing, (one of which was Yaro's two year old daughter), and the adults were eating, laughing, talking loudly, and waving at the camera. The shots of the interior of the buildings showed very little furniture on the dirt floors in the living/sleeping house. The rug on the wall was clearly a prized possession. The other building was a very basic kitchen. Water was pumped in by hand and if the cooking could be done outside, it was.

"My family will gather for a big celebration when I return next month. The whole village will be so happy." Did his eyes suggest he wouldn't be, Leisa wondered, or was that just what she wanted to think?

"So, how did you like my friends?" she asked as she was driving him back to the dorm.

"Ah, Diarabi (she loved this term of endearment)! They are all so beautiful and smart and happy. Jon too is a fine man. You are blessed to have such people in your life."

This was true. Leisa had several wonderful friends, especially women. How many times had she said that she found women to be more interesting than men? Maybe not so true any longer, she noted. However, accepting Yaro as a blessing in her life was a mixture of bliss and pain. Regardless of his confidence that destiny would eventually bring them together, reality dictated that they could only live in the moment. And how many books had she read that maintained that staying in the moment was the best guarantee for happiness anyway? Nevertheless, the day was fast approaching when he would leave her for his home and family. What then? Would she be able to sustain the feeling of gratitude for him having been in her life for only these few weeks? Sometimes she even entertained the notion that maybe she was finally being punished for not ever really being in love with anyone enough to put them before herself. Because at the age of forty two, she could honestly say that there wasn't a man alive she couldn't live without. But now this truth just might be history, she admitted to herself as she drove them towards Flagstaff. Never had she spent so much time examining who she was because of the man in her life.

The drive back to the university completed, she parked Shotsy and turned off her engine. She turned to stare at his dark face in the dark of night. She could not think of anything to say that would be encouraging in this moment.

"Don't despair, Diarabi. Remember that we can't know about this, so we waste our precious time together if we fill it with regret and doubts. For sure, I am not happy to leave you. You know that. I have seen the video many times, but today when I was watching it with your friends I experienced it differently. Melancholy entered my heart because it doesn't really feel like the life I want now.

34

Nevertheless, I am going back and it will be wonderful to see my family again. Yet, somehow you are part of my destiny. We must trust this mystery."

Days became weeks, and his departure for Burkina Faso was fast approaching. Yaro was a changed man, and the events of his life were the evidence of this. Her phone would ring with news of yet another invitation, and his exhilaration could be felt over the wires. There was a reception held in his honor at the home of his favorite college professor; the university arranged an over-night trip to Phoenix for him to meet other Fulbright scholars. He was the guest of honor at a farewell dinner party given by the Moslem men on campus, and most treasured of all were the private lunches or dinners with fellow students. Americans he had spent the past two years around, were now approaching him with conversation and invitations. "What is this, Diarabi? All this never before happened to me. Why now?"

Leisa had the answer. Close friends and family would testify that she usually did. She explained that this influx of activity was a natural evolution because of the change in his *spirit*, and this was being reflected in how people were relating to him now. The long months of no real human interaction had made him psychologically ill. His culture forbade him to seek hospitality, thus he was left alone for almost two years in the midst of humanity. He seemed to understand her theory which was based on her knowledge of transpersonal psychology. Because even our thoughts are energy, she clarified, what one experiences in the physical world is the result of one's habitual way of thinking. In his mind he had become a non-person, consequently, the world had experienced him as such.

And Leisa? Having been a student of herself for years, her analytical mind sought an answer for what she now realized was the most significant relationship of her life. Had she needed to recognize that she was prejudice or did it go beyond that? What about her habit of labeling men as appropriate or inappropriate? What about the concept that there are no accidents? What about the theory that the only control we have in this life is over what we do with the events that come our way? As the days slipped by, she journaled these ponderous questions that now held more than an academic interest for her.

Leisa spent considerable time selecting the place for their last time together. She knew that she would not be able to sit in the football stadium to watch him graduate. Neither did she want to be among the guests at the graduation party he was attending. She couldn't be one of the guests there to wish him well. No, they would take the Sunday afternoon before he left to return to Sedona. It had been the first place they had gone that Sunday in March, and it would now be their last.

"We are living in the moment, right?" Leisa asked as she headed Shotsy toward Sedona. How can a smile be both evidence of happiness and heartbreak at the same time, she wondered, as she turned to direct it at him.

"Ah yes, Diarabi. For sure, this is our time to be only now, together, with no future or past. Can we do it, you think?" Was his usual assurance forced, Leisa wondered.

"We will help each other", she replied as she drove the switchbacks through the canyon on this beautiful, late

Sunday afternoon. El Rincon Restaurante Mexicano, nestled in the splendor of Tlaquepaque Arts and Crafts Village in Sedona, was to be the scene of their last elaborate meal together. Leisa had chosen it for two reasons: it had the finest Mexican cuisine in all of Arizona, and number one rated margaritas since 1976. Yaro finally decided on two of their specialties: Navajo pizza for dinner and fruit chimichangas for desert. After dinner they spent an hour or so strolling through the shops to help their meal settle before driving back to the university.

As Leisa parked Shotsy near his dorm, he said "We must talk now, Diarabi, about what we do." His voice was as dark as the night that surrounded them.

"Yes, we need to make a plan we both can agree to." The car was warm, but there was a chill in her heart.

She continued, "I think we need to give ourselves over to our lives, and the only way we can do that is to not communicate with each other. You will be back with Anzounou and she deserves your whole heart and attention; your baby girl will want siblings, and your new position with the ministry of education will be demanding. You have spent almost all your life preparing for this, so now you must enjoy your destiny…to use your word."

There was a long silence and she could hear his breath coming short and irregular in the night. He reached for her hand and brought it to his lips. As he held it there and kissed her cupped palm she could hardly contain herself. Never had she experienced such passion. She loved this man like no other. But why? Nevertheless, nothing in her doubted this certainty now. She was completely, madly in love, and he was leaving. Leaving for his life in a world so foreign to her own. It made her heart ache for him to let go of her hand and back away. But he did.

Finally he responded to what she had said. "Okay. You are right, of course. But it will be me to break our silence. When the time is right, I will contact you. You will give me your daughter's phone number so she can be our way back to each other. Diarabi, I love you beyond measure, and we will meet again. For sure, you are part of my destiny. I will be back or you will come to my country. Whatever is Allah's design. You gave me back my life. I believe I would have died. I was almost dead that day in March when you took notice of me. I will love you all my days, and your memory will live in me across the many miles that will separate us for now."

CHAPTER THREE

Leisa had this easy, maddening way of making major life changes on a dime that drove her family and close friends crazy. This one would be no different, but as always, from her perspective, it was most welcomed and right on cue. She stretched and opened her eyes to see her bedroom. The bed, with its colorful, handmade quilt, white skirt and white decorator pillows was the room's main attraction. The gallery of framed family photographs hung above it. The big window on the opposite wall brought this 'most beautiful of worlds' into the large room. She had placed her desk in front of it with the computer she needed for her master's degree work. She was reclining in her favorite lounge chair, letting the feelings of peace wash over her, as she returned to full consciousness following her afternoon meditation.

She was in Sedona! A few weeks after Yaro left, she and Jon had moved to Sedona, into his beautiful home on Morgan Road. Now she could enjoy the red rocks by day, and the starry sky by night. The drive up through Oak Creek Canyon to her job at NAU in Flagstaff was a daily opportunity for inspiration. Ah yes, life's blessings. The extra activity around the move and the change of scene helped her live those first weeks of withdrawal. He was gone; there hadn't been or wouldn't be any communication, and no plan as to when they would see each other again. She knew that to argue with this reality would only continue her suffering. So if she wasn't going to wallow in misery, she would have to walk her talk. Being educated as to how to live one's life and doing it, are two different things. So now Leisa was getting an opportunity to see what she was made of. Had she really evolved into a more conscious person via years of reading and attending seminars and workshops on spiritual growth, or was it only a popular movement she joined, but didn't really embrace as a way of life? Her daily test now was, 'could she go forward with an attitude of thanksgiving for all the blessings in her life, and love what is'….and 'what is' is a life without Yaro.

Yes, she and Jon were very compatible under the same roof. That's why, when it became clear to him that he should return to his Sedona home (it was on the market, but hadn't sold yet), it was natural that she would continue there as his housemate. As she stretched her body some more and smiled at the beautiful bedroom, she mused about their relationship. Until Jon, Leisa had never lived around a man with whom she wasn't married or romantically involved. But it was clear to her that this arrangement was a major contributor to her sense of peace and well being, not to mention her pocketbook.

Anyway, she was all unpacked, settled in and ready to get on with this sunny day in July when she realized that Texas was on her mind. What? Return to Texas? This awareness was so 'off the wall' that her first reaction was to laugh out loud. Her voice startled her. Confounded, she settled back into the cushioned chair and gave her full attention to her thoughts. She had learned during the past five years in Arizona that her guides never used dramatics to communicate. They used her mind. The challenge had been to trust that it was her inner guidance and not her ego speaking.

And they were on a roll this afternoon: *You can't live on your NAU salary, thus your plastic debt is mounting with each month. You lack only six hours on your masters and now your boss says you can't take any classes this fall during the workday. You could have your Texas teacher's retirement in place in a few years, and like your brother has suggested, you might not want to work forever". You are missing your granddaughters' early years. Your dad has cancer and probably won't live much longer. Getting away from where you and Yaro were together will help you go on with your life without him.*

And Leisa's feelings? This deluge of mental activity had replaced her calm, still spirit with a wave of emotion. Vexed, she raised up off those cushions that encircled her and said, "Oh Shit! Not now! Not after just getting all my pictures hung yet again."

That silly objection was the only one she voiced or felt. Of course it was the thing to do. She knew it without even considering all that it entailed, so she got up and left her bedroom. As she walked down the long hall to Jon's huge, white kitchen she started organizing her return. By the time he got home, she had her plan on paper.

"Of course it makes sense Leisa, but doesn't it ever occur to you to take your time when making such life-altering decisions? Like a few days, at least?"

They were sitting on the deck, the sunset had stolen her heart, and she was only half listening to Jon. As she looked around at this Arizona world she loved so much, she kept waiting for the pain that always came with the idea of leaving it. But there wasn't any. No remorse, depression or upset, no nothing, so she looked at Jon and smiled.

"It's the thing to do. I know it is. Besides, I don't have time to wait. I'll have to give two weeks notice at NAU. That will put me back in Texas just in time for school to start. So I have plenty to think about. Like, what to do with my furniture? Do I go back to Houston where I last taught? Can I even get a teaching job at this late date? So come on Jon. Thank goodness I don't have to think about whether or not I'm doing the right thing." she said, still smiling, as she got up and gave him a hug. "Help me decide what to do with all my stuff, and how to tell my boss I'm out of here."

The highway was familiar: Phoenix, Tucson, Fort Stockton, San Antonio, Houston. Interstate 10 had seen her going both ways many times during the past five years, and this trip felt much like the first one she had made going west. Some of the circumstances were the same: no job; limited money; only a temporary place to live; scattered possessions. But this trip was different in a new way. Her heart was in it, but it wasn't as light as it habitually was. Today's reality was that Yaro was gone, yet without disavowing that fact, a small germ of disbelief insisted on wrapping itself around her life without him. All she could do was drive on.

"Put your mind on the future, Leisa," she said aloud to herself in a commanding voice. "Think about how lucky you are that Kitty answered the phone. You know how often times, she doesn't." So with hundreds of miles yet ahead of her, she did. As she drove east, she thought about Kitty Thomas. They went way back. Kitty was responsible for her getting a teaching job in Houston eight years earlier. Their interview had easily progressed beyond the professional topics to personal ones. Leisa had recognized her immediately as a major player in her life. They had kept in touch over the years with visits in her home every time she was back in Texas; a Christmas ski trip to Colorado, and Kitty had come to see her in Flagstaff. Now Leisa would be living with her until she could get a teaching job and get back on her feet financially. Was it only last week that she was trying to locate her?

After deciding to teach in Houston, she had called Kitty to ask if her offer to live with her anytime was still good. Since time was so short, Leisa was concerned when she didn't return her call. She knew that Kitty had just gotten a divorce and might be traveling, but where? How could she be reached in time? Nevertheless, for some strange reason Leisa didn't even consider contacting any of her other good friends in Houston. So the day the mail brought a letter from Kitty, she felt rewarded for following her guidance.

"Kitty! What possessed you to write me? I haven't heard from you in ages," were the first words out of her mouth when she got her on the phone.

"You always start conversation with a question, don't you Leisa? I don't know. I just got the urge to write you a 'having fun, wish you were here' kind of note. I certainly didn't expect a phone response, and did I actually put my son's phone number here in California in the letter?" The bubble in Kitty's voice was the same.

"No, you wrote it on the outside of the envelope…..on the back."

"Well, it must have been providential," Kitty laughed. "What's up?"

"I'm on my way back to Houston next week, and I need a teaching job and a place to live." Leisa said in her business-as-usual voice.

Kitty cracked up. Leisa could just see her rolling those big eyes and her dimples holding that famous smile. "Well, of course you can stay with me, but I don't know about any job openings. In-service days start in a couple of weeks, but I'm sure you realize that. Did I miss something? I didn't know you were coming back."

"Oh, I didn't know either until last week. You know how I am. I get the message and start packing." Leisa really didn't feel as confident as she sounded. Inner guidance or not, it was pretty scary.

"Leisa, your life is amazing. You are the only person I know who isn't afraid of 'what's next'. But hey! I don't worry about you for a minute. You always land on your feet. So by all means, come on down. I'll be home and it will be great to have some company. That big house is very lonely."

"So, how have you been? I know that you are divorced, but that's about all I know."

Leisa heard her sigh and a short silence answered her question. "I'm okay, I guess," she eventually said. "You were right. Do you remember telling me last year when you

44

were by to see me that if I didn't get out of that marriage, I was going to be very sick? Well, I did get sick. In fact, I almost died."

"Lord no, I didn't know anything about you being sick. But yeah, sure I remember saying that. However, that doesn't make me psychic. Anyone listening to your story would know that you couldn't go on living as you were and stay well. So, if you need someone to cheer your decision, you've got it. And that's not just because I need a roof over my head." laughed Leisa.

Kitty chuckled too. "Well, it's done. Right or wrong. But hey, I know we'll have a great time. I can't tell you how glad I am to know you're coming. We can be the 'Golden Girls', like on TV."

Yep! This is going to be good, she thought, as she ended her walk around a rest area and got back into Shotsy to finish the last stretch of the trip. She could just see them in Kitty's beautiful two story suburban home. Her own bedroom, bath, and study upstairs; burgers in the backyard; swims in the pool; Jacuzzi under the stars; book stores, theatre, shopping, and those late-night girl talks. She also realized that she wouldn't be able to talk to Kitty about Yaro, and that would be a good thing. Kitty was a world traveler and had even lived in Europe for a few years, but Leisa knew, even though the subject had never been discussed, that she would be shocked and disapproving of her love for a younger, married man from Africa. Bottom line.....Kitty had been born and raised in the South. So yes, no one in Texas would know about Yaro. Not Kitty or any other friend or her children.

"Looks like you are locking him away in your heart by moving back to where you can't possibly tell anyone about him. Do you suppose this has anything to do with your returning to Texas?" Like the tree outside her NAU office window, Shotsy didn't respond to her question either. She just kept on speeding down the highway towards Houston.

She hadn't actually lied, but she hadn't told the complete truth either and now she was paying for it. A position at Eisenhower High School teaching government and economics to seniors was one of the few ones left by the time Leisa hit Houston. She was afraid not to accept it even though she had never taught either subject. The administrator interviewing her just assumed that she had, since she was certified to teach social studies and had so many years' experience. But now after a month of a life almost exclusively made up of preparing lesson plans, she regretted letting her fear of not finding another teaching job, influence her to accept this one. Weekends were spent driving to her home town to visit her parents, and the week was nothing but solid school work. Not exactly what she had envisioned, but it did make time fly by. For sure (to use Yaro's phrase) that felt like a good thing.

The population of the school was predominately black. Imagine that! And, she loved teaching seniors. She hadn't lost her touch with teenagers either. The football players enjoyed flirting with her. "Miss! You're pimpin", she learned was a compliment. Maybe if she kept dressing real cool they wouldn't notice her difficulty explaining the legislative branch of the government.

Nothing in her life was anything like it had been in

Arizona. Houston traffic had replaced the magnificence of mountains, canyons, creeks, and an unpolluted sky. Instead of directing the student teacher program throughout the state, she now spent her days in a classroom with hormone driven teenagers. Weekends with elderly and ailing parents had replaced the company of an exotic man from across the world. And she knew that Kitty was disappointed that they didn't have more time together during the week. Leisa's habit was to stagger in the door at 4PM; take thirty minutes to escape into her TM; unceremoniously eat a frozen dinner; leave Kitty wanting to talk to go up the stairs to textbooks, and then fall into bed by 9:30. Kitty needed to talk about all the trauma she was living as a newly divorced woman, and Leisa just didn't have the time or the heart for it. The Golden Girls, they weren't!

And then there was the wreck! Driving in Houston was a daily flirt with death, so it wasn't a shock to be rear-ended. Leisa had always hated to wear a seat belt, so she usually didn't. However, she did pay attention to her gut feelings, so as she was leaving the parking lot of a grocery store one day she had the thought to buckle up. A few minutes later she was within a block of her apartment when an old tank of a Buick rammed her from behind. The force was so great that it broke all of her long fingernails as she clung to Shotsy's steering wheel. Certainly, she would have gone through the windshield had she not had the seat belt on. All in all, the whole incident wasn't too bad. The police were there immediately; the driver of the old Buick was ticketed for tailgating; the wrecker guy suggested a good body shop for Shotsy; her State Farm Insurance provided for a rental car and it was delivered in short order, and she wasn't in pain yet, so the phone call to her daughter wasn't too alarming. Nevertheless, the next morning when she woke up with neck and back pain, and she was so sore that she couldn't get out of bed – the accident took on a different flavor.

Shotsy was critically hurt. The trunk of the car was pushed to the back of the front seat, thus she was in the repair shop for two weeks. Leisa was hurt too. Two herniated discs in her neck had her sporting a neck brace to class, and this diagnosis required the attentions of a chiropractor. Now, the only up side to all this was that the doctor turned out to be a retired professional football player with all the right stuff. He was tall, handsome, drove a Corvette, liked to dance, and his brother was a friend of Kitty's. However, since she drove to Nacogdoches every weekend to see her parents, and dating during the week wasn't even an option – nothing much came of the attraction. Once in a while, after a treatment, he would ask her to join him for an early dinner at Joe's Crab Shack, (next door to his office), but that was about it. He did take her to the Homecoming Dance and that got her points with her students. Actually, once Leisa got past the externals, there was really nothing to entertain as a possibility. She had to go for adjustments twice a week, thus it didn't take long for her to realize that he was a great package, but nothing more. Icing yes, but since she didn't have room in her life for a man, it wasn't painful to not give it a shot. Besides, being around him brought back memories of Yaro, and that didn't make for a happier day.

* * * * *

Her dad had always worked away from home. Consequently they had never been close, yet she knew that he loved her very much. Now that his tall, strong body was becoming more and more bent and frail, the weekends they spent together were most precious to Leisa. Her 85 year old dad had become the man in her life.

A pattern was established as the fall months passed. She would leave from school on Fridays and drive north for three hours through East Texas piney woods to the oldest town in Texas - Nacogdoches. That was her birthplace and her family had returned to live there when she was in high school. All but one or two of her best friends had stayed after graduation to attend Stephen F. Austin University as she did. Those college years had been the happiest of her young life. She never missed one dance held every Thursday night at the Student Union Building, so the main criteria for a boyfriend was - he must enjoy dancing.

Leisa would get to her parent's apartment sometime around 7o'clock and her dad would note the exact time and comment. "Well, the traffic must have been okay, daughter. It's 7:05. Are you ready for that drink?" They would sit and visit while she enjoyed her scotch and soda before leaving for the catfish place, as her dad called it. He could always find the best places to eat, and this mom and pop joint was out a country road a few miles from town. "Are you going with us tonight, Hon?" was his every-Friday question to his wife.

"No, I don't like the people who go there and you know it. Just bring me a plate when you come back" was her every-time answer. This exchange always prompted Leisa to pray silently that she hadn't inherited too large a dose of her mother's habit of faultfinding.

The three hour drive back to Houston every Sunday became the only time she allowed herself to think about her days with Yaro in Flagstaff. She did have a few photos with him in them, but she didn't look at them often. No picture was needed to remember every thing about him, so on Sundays she would revisit their times together as she drove Shotsy south. As the weeks became months, the heartbreak lessened, but the longing remained. Gradually, she realized, she was moving in her mind to Yaro's claim that destiny would bring them back together again. Was it just a way to make the moment more bearable, or did she really believe it? Never one to give much reliance on miracles (and their lives coming together would certainly be one), she tried not to spend too much energy on 'how this could happen'. Instead, at night she would put herself to sleep visualizing what her life would be like with Yaro as her husband. Because she didn't want to be so far away from her children, her fantasies were always set in the United States; in some northern state (because of the race thing), and in a cosmopolitan city. It made her happier to do this, so she did. Whether the books were right or not about visualizing what you want, she wasn't sure. But, it didn't cost anything, and what if it did have some affect? Never one to discount something just because it couldn't be proved, prompted her to spend time visualizing the life she would love with the person she loved.

Eventually the Nacogdoches routine of her dad driving them to WalMart to buy groceries; to the barbeque place for lunch; out to the cemetery to admire the spot near the tree where he would be buried, and over the country roads of his youth was replaced with visits confined to the apartment. Hospice had ordered a hospital bed and it was in the living room. Now they spent the weekends with his favorite memories: southern meals of biscuits and red-eye gravy, catfish and hush puppies, chicken fried steak with mashed potatoes; his adventures across Texas while building highways; the early retirement years spent seeing the country on his Harley motorcycle, and all about his favorite cars (of the many he had owned), and the best roads to travel. Leisa was sure she had gotten her love of the open road from her dad. She liked to say that her blood was half gasoline like his. One would think that he would lose his passion for living now that he didn't want one bite of anything to eat, and he could no longer walk out to his Chrysler and drive it anywhere he wanted to go. But no, even on the day before he died he was interested in the selection of the prettiest housecoat in Nacogdoches for his wife's birthday.

The large parlor in the funeral home was packed. All of his many friends were there, and his relatives came from all over the state to pay homage. Having attended so many funerals in the past few years, he knew exactly what he wanted, therefore he had planned it all. The men in his Sunday school class were the honorary pallbearers, but his six grandsons did the actual honors. The sermon was short, the songs were the traditional Baptist ones, and Leisa managed to give a short talk she felt sure he loved. However, the surprise of the day was learning that their dad's plan included treating all of his children, grandchildren and great grandchildren to a meal together at 'the catfish place' following his burial.

CHAPTER FOUR

Shotsy was headed in a different direction now on most weekends. Since the death of her father, her mother had been moved to her brother's hometown, thus there was no longer any reason to drive northeast to Nacogdoches. Instead, it was a two hour drive west from Houston towards San Antonio, back to the small ranching community where she had raised her children.

Being in a car alone to drive two or three hours was a constant in Leisa's life. Last fall it had been back to her youth every weekend. Her home town with classmates she reconnected with, and being around her parents gave her a perspective of herself she hadn't considered in decades. Being a closet psychologist, this revisiting the past gave her plenty of material to analyze and pose to her car, Shotsy. Now it was spring, and the players and scene was a different story. The eighteen years as a rancher's wife was front and center in her mind as she retraced the events of her adult past. It would appear that destiny was aiding her by keeping the memories of Yaro not the constant daily fare that they might have been. "That's how he would think of it, isn't it Shotsy?" She asked aloud as she turned onto Interstate 10 headed west. "Since you never answer me, I know that all my secrets are safe with you." Leisa laughed and patted her dash. Yes, the open road invited introspection, and there was much to remember.

All those many years of teaching in a small town and raising her family on the ranch were good times. Her children had been successful as teenagers and had moved into young adulthood without incident. Her ex-husband's kind heart and loving ways, packaged in a tall, slim, handsome body made him undeserving of divorce court. Her career as an outstanding teacher was well documented. She had married into an unsophisticated, rural South Texas community, where walking around the courthouse square on a Saturday afternoon brought sounds of German, Bohemian, and the broken English of ranchers in town doing their shopping, beer drinking and domino playing. She had been a big fish in a small pond, and life was good. But her happiness diminished with the years.....once she got past the babies, building the new ranch house, and the first of several exotic vacations. Gradually, underneath her interest in sticks and bricks and social activities was an emptiness that went unnamed for the last six of the eighteen year marriage. Given her life circumstances, she didn't have a leg to stand on. Acknowledging the lackluster in her life would have been sacrilege.

When did it all begin? Why did she choose to leave her home and family? What was she looking for? What didn't she have? The events and feelings of those last years at the ranch revealed only that nothing, absolutely nothing, brought the joy of being alive to her heart any more. A new life was beckoning to her. But why?

"So Shotsy, what do you think? Everything I read indicates that problems are really gifts in disguise. If that is so, then my unhappiness in all its forms back then was for the purpose of getting me to change. I can't prove this, but I resonate with the idea that a person creates their reality with their habitual way of thinking. You didn't know me then, but for years I found fault with my marriage, the teachings of my church, and the administration of the school district in which I taught. Now today, I think I was wrong to feel victimized. Maybe there is another way to see pain and problems, besides as pain and problems. That would certainly help me with my life right now, wouldn't it? Come on Shotsy, break your silence and agree with me because if I can manage to believe that my love for Yaro is not a problem, but a blessing in my life, I can feel happiness today, tomorrow and the next day. Okay, okay. Happiness is a stretch. I'll settle for peace. Might I manage peace?" Leisa was glad to see that they were only about 15 miles from the ranch because, for sure, (as Yaro would say), Shotsy wasn't talking to her.

She called them her sunshine girls. Her two tall-for-their-age, blond, beautiful granddaughters who were five and three years old, loved to see Shotsy pull up on a late, Friday afternoon. Many times they would be together flying across the pasture in their little pink jeep Santa had brought, with the several dogs barking and running along side. Her son and daughter lived next to each other at the south end of the family ranch, so she was home to both families easily. What a welcomed change it was for Leisa, at least twice a month now her weekends were filled with fishing trips, playing poker at Grandpa's house with her granddaughters, family holidays, deer camp gatherings, and good ole country dancing at the local community center. The father of her children was the best dancer in the county, and once in a while they would go dancing together. That is, whenever his current lady friend could be allowing of their relationship. Needless to say, it didn't happen too often. The happy, healthy people, the sounds and smells of the country, and the pure delight of being around her granddaughters were balm for her spirit. Leisa probably needed them much more than they needed her. However, they would not have guessed why.

Life in Houston was on the upswing too. It must have been her guardian angles who interceded and brought the change of teaching assignment at mid-semester. Leisa was now teaching American History instead of government and economics. With this familiar subject she no longer had to spend long hours struggling with how to teach government to seniors. Consequently, she and Kitty were becoming the 'Golden Girls' at last. And like the TV characters, their conversations most often revolved around the subject of men and the mystery of relationships.

"I don't care what you say Leisa, I am telling you right now that I am never going to get involved with a man again." Kitty was cleaning the pool and interrupting Leisa's plan to nap in the sunshine. Kitty continued, "Of course it helps if I have someone to talk to while I do this, so open your eyes and listen to me. But seriously, I am not at all sure I understand or like what you say about intimate relation-ships. To begin with, what makes you think they have to have an evolutionary purpose?"

"Oh, I don't know", Leisa said lazily as she opened her eyes. The May sunshine was inviting her to nap, but the least she could do was talk to Kitty. She would be moving into her own apartment when school was out, so it wouldn't be as easy and often to visit like this. "It just seems to me that we learn the most about ourselves from the people who are the major players in our lives." She sat up and looked at Kitty. "Do you really want to discuss this or are you just looking for an argument?" laughed Leisa. "If you are serious, I'll go in the house and get Daphne Rose Kingma's book, *The Future of Love*. I don't want you to think that the concepts I espouse are original with me. Nope, I'm just one of many who is looking for a better way to show up for life."

"Sure, go get it. I'm about finished with this week's pool cleaning so I'll make us some tea and then I'll be your Saturday student." Kitty cocked her head to one side and smiled a smile that said 'You are too much'.

"We are relational beings. Any argument there?" Leisa said with a sigh as she settled into her favorite lounge chair with the book and the tea Kitty offered.

"Now don't treat me like the village idiot. Of course, we are relational beings. My problem is with your claim that the people we attract into our lives have to do most with what it is we need to learn about ourselves. My experience has been that they destroy my life, over and over. So why wouldn't I be better served to never get into another romantic relationship?"

Leisa nodded her head and explained, "According to this book, we are intuitively drawn to the person who has what we don't have, what we lost, what got hurt, or was never developed in childhood. So we establish a relationship with someone and stay connected to that person because we want to develop that missing component in ourselves. Let's use me as an example. I don't have the willingness to allow for difference, and although all the books demand it, I can't seem to come from a position of unconditional love with my mates. If they can't dance; read the books I do; enjoy everything from opera to playing dominos in Shiner, Texas; engage in long hours of analyzing behavior, or are willing to start a whole new life some place else – on a dime, then they have failed the test and I must move on. Consequently, I have attracted man after man who doesn't meet all my requirements (like there is one who could). Yet, none of them have demanded that I be like them, in fact, my differences are attractive to them. So bottom line, they have had the unconditional love for me that I haven't had for them. Therefore, I will keep attracting these men until I change who I am. It isn't about them, it is about me."

Kitty was silent and it was obvious that she was considering this in light of her own life. She couldn't tell by looking that Leisa's thoughts had left her and sped to another continent. This conversation had brought Yaro to her instantly. He was black, thus she had convicted him of not being appropriate for her. Somehow his race had been more repellent than the fact that he was also married and much younger. They mattered, but she didn't have an emotional reaction to them. She had initially let the color of his skin convict him as not suitable, before she even had a clue as to what manner of man he was.

Kitty finally responded, "Okay, I can see why you

could apply this theory to your life, but I don't see how it relates to mine. Can you tell me why all the men in my life, beginning with my dad, have treated me like shit? They all have, every damn one of them, been unappreciative of my love and they didn't value who I was. There was always some criticism: I needed to lose weight; I needed to be on time; I needed to change the way I dressed or wore my hair; I needed to give them more space, I needed to, I needed to, I needed to." Kitty's voice got louder and angrier with each word.

Leisa was half-way sorry they were having this conversation, but she plunged on. "It seems to me Kitty, that from what I know about your life, you have spent it trying to please in order to feel loved. Beginning with your dad, you have swallowed a shit-load of abuse all your life. You taught all these men how to treat you by excusing their degrading behavior because you needed their love. Therefore, these men are a mirror for you. They reflect the way you think about yourself. If you had healthy love and respect for yourself, you wouldn't allow them to mistreat you in the hopes of getting the love you want. My favorite definition for insanity is, 'To keep doing what you are doing, yet expect a different result'. If you are ever going to get past this way of being in relationships, you have to be in one. That's why I say that you and I have to be in romantic relationships if we are to ever change the way we have always been. It's like getting back into the saddle once we realize there is a better way to ride."

Leisa was glad to see Kitty get up and pick up her empty glass of tea. "Let me digest this a while, Leisa

Divine. I'll leave you to your book or a nap in the sunshine. What I need most right now is a shower." That nickname was the most ridiculous one anyone had ever given her, thought Leisa, as she watched Kitty close the back door.

Kitty's departure left Leisa alone with her memories. She had learned during these past nine months to not let the tape run whenever it wanted to. Instead she had established the routine of having a 'Yaro Time' when the time was right, and that was usually about once a week. She would go with whatever subject had brought him forth. Maybe it was reliving their conversations, or maybe it was speculation on what might yet be, or maybe it was the purpose or point of it all, like today.

She was flipping through the book she had already read to reread passages she had highlighted.

"....In relationship we go through experiences that show us who we are, how we are broken, and how we need to be mended...God wants us to wake up now. God wants us to know each other as spirits as well as personalities, to embrace our lives as the exquisite spiritual journeys they are, and to deliver us from the tedious, frustrating, and ultimately unsatisfying ordeals that our relationships become when we live them only at the personality level....

.....Intimate relationship is the ultimate container of love in the human experience....Life is not a problem. It is a miracle, a gift, a teaching, a celebration.....Every psychological issue is also a spiritual teaching in opening our hearts, for how we deal with the issue emotionally is always a step toward our spiritual selves.....We are eternal spirits who have stepped into life with a grand and specific

purpose: to be able to love without limitation".

Could it possibly be that because she had failed to change her fault-finding ways with the men who came before, she had attracted Yaro into her life because of all the unacceptables a relationship with him would entail? Since she hadn't learned to not try to change all the others to fit her needs, she was given a man with two out of three things that couldn't be changed: race and age.

"Give it a rest, Leisa," she said aloud to herself as she shut the book and closed her eyes. "Put yourself to sleep by fantasizing his arms around you and his lips on yours. Your way of analyzing yourself, him and your relationship wears me out. Nap time, please."

* * * * *

The new apartment was so totally hers. Kitty's home was gorgeous and she had been comfortable there, but when tears came as she was unpacking her set of pink towels and framed family pictures, she realized how starved she was for her own space and stuff. The apartment had two bedrooms and two baths. Room for visitors! And, the swimming pool was a way to keep her stock up with the two sunshine granddaughters. Their grandmother was adding another dimension to their lives. On the ranch it was all about horses, fishing, and hunting. Now, their Houston weekends meant going to the Alley Theatre to see both musicals and comedies; touring the museums and space center for a broader view of the world, and the shopping sprees at the gigantic malls had them convinced that Gran's purse was always full of money.

Between Kitty's friends and the new ones she had made at work, Leisa had a fun circle of folks to do weekends with. If she wasn't at the ranch, she had endless entertainment opportunities in Houston. Friday nights were always spent at the Red River Dance Hall where she danced and enjoyed the happy hour hot buffet with her friends from school. There was no such thing as being lonely, but there was a vacancy in her heart that was growing as the years passed. Her habit was to come home from work and once out of her panty hose and bra, she would retire to the fully furnished covered patio with a glass of wine. It was the perfect place to relax, and if it hadn't been for the temptation to smoke a cigarette, it would have been tension free, if not content.

As Leisa would watch the sun setting through the tall pine trees (she was so fortunate to have found an apartment complex built without removing the trees), her thoughts would return to Flagstaff. It wasn't painful now, instead it was a mixture of delight and melancholy. Thank goodness the scenes don't get worn out with time, she thought, as she selected one to relive. Seldom did she wonder about Yaro's life now. All she had ever done was to look up Burkina Faso on the web, just to have some frame of reference. However, since she could not see him in that setting, she ended the effort to. He would remain in her heart as the student at NAU. For sure (as he would say) her mind had lost out to her heart, and that had never happened before or since.

There had been opportunities to date and she had. Actually she was living her philosophy that men are only icing. Her cake was wonderful: her own darling apartment; weekends with her children and grandchildren; a huge city with an endless supply of restaurants, things to do, and people to do them with; teaching teenagers was never boring, and no one believed her age. There were men too that showed up on a regular basis. Since she was not looking for a committed relationship and they could figure out right quick that she wasn't needy, they found her very desirable. Leisa enjoyed the interaction with these men, and she valued her ability to attract really great ones, but none of them ever made it into her heart. There was seldom any trauma/drama around her dating. Whenever the man pressed for more, it was over. To protect from feeling guilty, she was always very diligent in making it clear from the very first date, that a casual relationship without an agenda was her plan. Sometimes, however, during the week when she was sitting alone on her patio trying not to smoke a cigarette, she would analyze her behavior. The only thing she could conclude was that there was this denied belief, deep inside of her, that Yaro was her destiny. She would chuckle at the word, destiny. Unlike him, she wasn't at all sure about such. Nevertheless, there was this something in her that kept her emotionally tied to a man she might never see again. "I wonder if this is to be my punishment for not getting it right with any of the others?",she often wondered, out loud, to no one.

She still talked to herself. As she picked up her empty wine glass and opened the screen door, she said one last thing to the approaching night, "I can wait forever because I love my life."

CHAPTER FIVE

How can a person be happy and miserable all at the
same time? He didn't know, but as Yaro's plane flew long
hours crossing the ocean, he had plenty of time to experience
it. As he tried to sleep, read or watch the movie being shown
to the passengers, his mind did battle with his heart. Leisa
would have been surprised to see how upset and unsure he
was. Speeding across the sky away from her had him
questioning his fate.

Everything had always been as needed in his life.
That is, before Leisa. He had found an educated woman to
marry, and it was a good choice for them both. The fact that
there had never been consuming passion between them he
had dismissed as the normal way of it. They had the same
goals; he was proud of her beauty; she was a very calm and
capable person; there were seldom any surprises in their
domestic life, and their mutual respect for each other created
the space they both wanted for their lives as individuals.

Too, winning the Fulbright Scholarship had been
right on schedule. He could have settled for getting his post
graduate degree there in Ouagadougou at the university, but
he knew that it was not as prestigious as a master's degree
from an American school. Consequently, after they married,
he taught school for five years while he studied at night and

on weekends for the exam. Studying was a way of life for him and had been since he was a young boy. It was not a burden; in fact, he had always experienced it as a blessing. He had been chosen. His parents had chosen him and not any of his five brothers, and with that one decision his entire life had been drastically altered. Now he was returning to continue fulfilling his obligation to his large family. He would be so proud to send money to his parents, more now than ever before. And this was just the beginning. He was confident that he would achieve prominence in the field of education. In a few years a PhD would be needed, and then his preparation to be highly placed in his country's educational ministry would be complete.

Yes, events today would be as anticipated and dreamed of had it not been for Leisa. His plane was over Africa now and he would soon be back into familiar surroundings. The family, friends, home, foods, culture, and geography he had been born to. As he stared out the window at the clouds, he allowed the tears because they must not continue. As a devotee to Allah, he would trust and wait. At this time, there was nothing he could do with this love. It would live in his heart and provide the memories that would not grow dim. Until it was time to put their lives together, he would not contact Leisa. Their agreement to not communicate was a sound one. As individuals, on the opposite sides of the world, they would both go on with their lives. He could do this thing. He must. As the plane was taxiing on the Ouagadougou runway, he gathered the gifts he had for his wife and child, and surrendered to his destiny.

"There, over there. Ana, that's your papa. Run give

him a hug," Anazounou instructed her daughter, but the four year old clung to her mother's skirt and refused to budge.

Yaro saw his wife and waved. "Ah! My two beautiful ladies", he called as he rushed to them.

Did he not even kiss her? Instead, without any plan to do it he just quickly put his arms around her and held her to his chest in a long, loving embrace. With his eyes closed and his arms holding her tight he could feel Ana squirming between them.

"Welcome home, my husband. It will take Ana a little time. She doesn't remember you," Anzounou whispered before she left his arms and raised her head to look into his eyes.

"Oh, for sure. I understand her shyness. Come, let me look at you Ana. I am your Papa. Remember how you talked to me on the phone while I was away from you and Mama to go to school?" That seemed to help because her reluctance to look at him diminished a little. Encouraged, Yaro continued, "Yes, my goodness, you have grown to be such a big girl, and you will be going to school too before long." With that, Ana came away from behind her mother; however, she still would not look directly at Yaro or talk to him. But he could see her. "Oh Anzounou, she is going to be tall like you. And her eyes, look at her magnificent almond eyes and lush eyelashes. What a beauty you are Ana. Come, tell me about your hair style."

"Yes, Ana, tell Papa how long it took us to get all those ribbons properly placed in your long, curly hair," urged Anzounou, but to no avail. She wisely took the pressure off her daughter by looking at Yaro and saying in a teasing way,

65

"….and how about your other girl? What have the past two years done to me?"

Yaro just beamed at her for the astute way she was helping an awkward moment. Yes, Anzounou was a beauty, but he had been more attracted to her sage spirit and judicious ways than to her flawless body. Nothing ever seemed to rattle her. She approached life with a confidence born of an unusual circumstance for a woman in Burkina Faso. Unlike most young women, she had not married early. Instead, she had gotten a teaching degree in home economics and had been a career woman for three years before they had married. She hadn't blinked an eye to be left alone with their two year old daughter, Ana, while he was in America getting his master's degree. No, Anazounou was a good match for whatever life brought. He loved and respected her for that.

Nothing had changed. His home was exactly as he had left it, but now that he was back and his salary would be greater, some improvements would be made. Although family ties were strong, individuals actually were quite independent, so their buying a house when they first married was an important benchmark. It needed better plumbing and some remodeling, but owning a less-than-perfect house was better than renting something nicer. With the coming years, it would be transformed into a home they both could be proud of.

Almost as soon as they walked in the door, friends and neighbors started arriving to see Yaro. He had just given his wife and daughter their gifts when he heard them announcing their presence by saying, (if they were Moslem), *Salaam ale kum* (peace be upon you) to which he would reply *Ale kum Salaam* (and peace to you), as a way of inviting the visitors in. People who weren't Moslem would announce their arrival by clapping their hands (instead of knocking) or saying ko,ko,ko. The guests were offered a place to sit and water to drink. Refusing to drink is socially inappropriate, even if one is not thirsty. Eventually, Anzounou left the men to their visiting and tea-making because it is an important social ritual among them. It can take half an hour to prepare each of the three rounds of tea on a bed of charcoal, the third round being the weakest brew.

After getting Ana to sleep, they found themselves actually alone for the first time since he had gotten off the plane. The sun was down, but it was still really warm so the cool shower refreshed Yaro. Anzounou didn't join him, of course. That was not their habit or accepted way. As he came to bed, she smiled and said, "So, husband. You are back."

There were no inquires about how he felt. There would be no leading questions about what he was thinking. Instead, she accepted his love making in silence and if she noticed that it was without much appetite, it would never be spoken of. They had never intruded into each other's feelings, so nothing was unusual. He was tired and emotionless. After giving his wife a goodnight pat on her cheek, he moved over to be alone with his memories. Maybe in sleep, he hoped, Leisa would come.

It took five hours on the riverboat to get to his parent's village of Burkinabe. What a culture shock it was for Yaro. It was hard for him to accept that he was on the same planet. Instead of highways with eighteen wheelers racing by, he watched the elephants as the boat moved slowly down the river. For sure, he observed, elephants are the architects of the forest. In their daily rounds of feeding, drinking, and socializing they create trails and clearings, which the rains may turn into streams and water holes. As the river took him further and further away from the city, the rural culture returned him to the memories of his youth. The general attitude of his people was warm, friendly and generous. Honesty, wisdom and loyalty are valued, as well as the ability to control one's tongue. As he sat still with his gaze on the riverbank or on the other people in the boat with him and his family, he used this idle time to recall the character-istics of the people of Burkina Faso (a name that means 'the land of upright and courageous people'). Even though he was in a very primitive country compared to the United States, it made him proud that his countrymen have strong family values centered on sharing and on respect for customs and tradition. The elderly are highly respected. Young people are expected to do whatever older relatives, teachers, or neighbors ask. Humility and generosity are the most desired personal traits, while bragging is least tolerated.

In rural settings, men wear a Muslim robe (boubou) while women wear a wraparound skirt (pagne) with a blouse or T-shirt. Both rural and urban dwellers buy used clothing imported from Europe, Asia, and the United States. This is why Yaro had known to shop at the Goodwill store there in Flagstaff for suits before his return. However, as civic leaders call for consumption of local products, embroidered traditional outfits have become more popular attire for social events. Women often have elaborate hairstyles and change them every few months. Even Anzounou used braided extensions, wigs and 'spikes' of hair (made by wrapping hair with black thread). It was no longer as common in the city, but Yaro noticed that two women who joined them on the trip up river had traditional face scarring. They were probably members of the Mossi or Bwaba tribes, he concluded.

Rural families, like his family, often live in a compound, with separate sleeping quarters for men and women. A mother generally cares for her children until they are weaned at around age three. At this time, boys move from sleeping in the mother's house to sleeping in the father's house. Both boys and girls are cared for by their parents until they reach adulthood, but boys generally receive more support than girls. Once girls marry, they are perceived as having changed families.

In polygamous families, wives share chores, including cleaning the courtyard and preparing family meals. Rural women have few property rights and can be sent back to their families if their husbands are unsatisfied with them. In matriarchal families women have more rights. In urban settings, women are more often educated and able to find jobs. That was why Anzounou was so different from the women in his village. She had been born and raised in Ouagadougou, thus her family had educated her to be independent of a husband. Therefore, when they met at work, (both being teachers at the same public school), they were free to date and to marry. This is becoming the norm in urban areas; however, marriages in the countryside are usually still arranged. He remembered that his six sisters' marriages were all arranged by his parents. He hoped they were happy because the only way out of an arranged marriage was to run away. And as far as Yaro knew, none of his brothers-in-law had other wives. He realized that Islamic laws allowed a man to have as many as four wives, but in urban centers due to the cost of raising and educating a family, it wasn't as common as in rural areas.

Anzounou had not been to visit Yaro's parents while he was away, and they had only seen Ana during her first year. She was a city woman, thus it was not expected. As Yaro glanced at his wife who was entertaining their daughter, he speculated about whether or not he should refresh her memory about rural courtesies. No doubt she remembered, but she might appreciate a review lesson. He had time, and so he would before they got to his village, but not now because mother and daughter were enjoying playing together. Ana still wasn't sure of him so he continued to sit apart from them, turning his thoughts from his family to his culture.

Rural customs for Burkinabe were rather involved. He remembered that before engaging in any social activity, one takes the time to greet and shake hands. Greetings include inquiries about family, health, and work. One may show respect by bowing one's head. Or when shaking hands, one might touch the other's right hand or arm at the elbow level with one's left hand. Male friends may touch their right fists to their hearts after shaking hands. In the countryside, women may kneel to express respect. In Muslim settings, like in Yaro's village, men often will not shake hands with women, as Islamic principles dictate

70

minimal contact between unrelated men and women. Not greeting all those in a room or at a table is considered rude.

He would have to remember to remind Anzounou about accepted gestures too. Sometimes in the city these old ways aren't always honored, but in the country they are still very important. For example, use the right hand to greet people, pass items and eat. Using the left hand, especially for greeting or eating is offensive. Men and women hold hands in public with friends of the same gender, but displays of affection between men and women are inappropriate. To motion to someone using the index finger is considered disrespectful; instead, one motions with the palm of the hand down. It is rude to call someone's name unless the person is nearby. If the person is farther away, it is polite to whistle or make a loud *psst* sound in order to get his or her attention. No doubt Anzounou will recognize the more common rural Burkinabe way of expressing disgust at events or actions by rounding the lips and making a noise by sucking air through the front teeth.

He was sure a great feast was being planned, and he knew that his wife would need some coaching with this. Food is not treated casually and meals are eaten in general silence. In his village, the men will eat together in a circle on the floor, sharing a common platter and using the fingers of the right hand. Using the left hand is forbidden. Anzounou and Ana will join the other women and children to eat together in a different section of the compound. Guests must take at least a few bites or risk offending the host. This arrangement will be odd to Anzounou because urban families tend to eat together, and they use a dining table and utensils more often than their rural counterparts. However, she will enjoy the fact that both cities and villages usually have dolo cabarets, (local drink stands), tended by women, where both men and women gather for drinks, food, and discussion of local events and gossip.

He was sure his wife had not eaten *t^o* since they were last in his village. *T^o* is Burkina Faso's main staple - sorghum, millet, or corn flour cooked into a hard porridge. Rural people usually eat it twice a day with a variety of sauces made from peanuts and indigenous plants and vegetables, such as sorrel and okra. And a rural breakfast usually consists of leftovers from the previous night. He was sure that Anzounou would have trouble with this. At home fresh fruit was her favorite morning meal.

Yaro could tell from a distance that his village was in a celebrating mood. As it happened, his baby brother, Errou, and his companions had just brought the cattle safely to the banks of the Mouhoun River after a long and arduous trek through the grasslands. Yaro remembered that it was a tough job, walking from sunrise to sunset. The men get so thirsty and the cows get tired, but you constantly have to find new grazing so you move on because your mission is to bring back fat cattle. The wealth and identity of the village are invested in its cattle. The men from the village watch as Errou and the other young men plunge into the river with hundreds of animals. Yaro knows how dangerous it is to be in the water swimming with cattle, and trying to keep them apart so they don't get injured. It is a great day for Errou because his girl friend, Ica Bar, is there on the bank watching too. His chances of marrying her depend very much upon

72

how well he has looked after the herd. He needs for his cattle to be the fattest and most beautiful. It warmed Yaro's heart to watch his baby brother emerge from the river with his cattle all safe and sound. Yes, these two sons, both very accomplished and successful, kneeled together at their mother's feet to pay homage to the woman who had given them life. Two very different men whose recent worlds could not be compared, were celebrated in unison under the stars that evening in the village of their youth.

There was feasting, music, dancing, and so many questions for Yaro. Everyone wanted to know about America and Americans. Thank goodness he could give a happy report, courtesy of those last two months after he had met Leisa. Did anyone notice? Several times, when he was about to tell a story, he would open his mouth to share a description of Lake Powell, Sedona, or the Grand Canyon only to shut it again because the memory was wrapped around Leisa. He felt schizophrenic and he sensed that his wife was aware of it. However, nothing in her smile or approving nods betrayed her thoughts. If she suspected that he was omitting events, places, or people, that was his right and it was not her place to question. She knew that he loved and respected her, and that was what she cared about. They had been happy and comfortable with each other before he left, and they are today and will continue to be. Their future will be what they had planned together.

It had been a happy reunion, and his mother had seemed especially thrilled with the earrings he had given her. Leisa had helped him know where to shop for the earrings and the large handled knife that he presented to his father.

73

Now they were on their way back to Ouagadougou so his thoughts turned to his new job at the university. His country was in great need of educational advance, and he was to be a part of that process. Their educational system was based on the French model. Therefore, mastery of the French language largely determined one's success because all instruction was in French. Since young children starting school have no French background, they do not understand or learn well. It was not so difficult for him, he remembered, but for most it was. Elementary school lasts six years; secondary has seven years. Classes can be extremely large. Primary enrollment is estimated at 36 percent; about one-fourth of these students go on to the secondary level, as he did. Many students drop out because they can no longer afford school fees. All rates are lower for girls and rural students, and that is why his family was able to keep him in the boarding school. Entrance to one of the country's three universities is available to those who pass difficult exams; usually only a small percentage passes. He could still remember those long hours over his books, but as always, his good study habits were rewarded with diplomas and degrees. As he watched the low flying white birds dip into the river water, he knew that one more degree was needed. How long would it take him to get another opportunity to return to the United States for his PhD? And the other question that followed on its heel this late afternoon in June....would he see Leisa then?

CHAPTER SIX

By the time they had gotten off the boat and back to their home in Ouagadougou, it was time for his evening prayers. Salah, the ritual prayer practiced by Muslims in supplication to Allah, was primarily to act as an individual's communion with Allah. It enables one to stand in front of God, thank and praise Him, and ask for Him to show one the 'right path'. In addition, the daily ritual prayers serve as a constant reminder to Muslims that they should be grateful for God's blessings. It ensures that every Muslim prioritizes Islam over all other concerns, thereby revolving their life around God and submitting to His will. Prayer also serves as a formal method of remembering God. Tonight, Yaro felt more need for divine participation in his life than usual. He had four reasons for this: he was nervous about starting his new job at the university tomorrow; he longed for Ana to be comfortable around him again; he wanted his wife to be happy with him and their life together, and he must have some relief from the longing he had for Leisa. He had been taught that Allah could answer all prayers. Those were his.

As he rode his bicycle to the university, he could see changes in this city of over a million. Most of its inhabitants were like him this morning, on their motorcycles or bicycles. As he peddled himself towards the university he noticed that there had been an increase in the number of hotels and restaurants, and there were now more four and five star hotels available. Anzounou had told him that communications and media had contributed significantly to the development of Ouagadougou in the last two years. Local state-funded media had been boosted, as city council members were trying to address problems, such as poor health care, prostitution, low literacy, and high criminality rates. To tackle these issues, the population's awareness needed to be raised. As a result, the media's importance had increased.

Since Yaro was early, he decided to stop for a rest in Bangr-Weoogo Park. It was a well known site in Ouagadougou, and he and Anzounou had gone there often when they were dating. Before colonialism, it belonged to the Mosse chiefs. Considering it a sacred forest, many went there for traditional initiations or for refuge. The French colonists, disregarding its local significance and history, established it as a park in the 1930s. In 1985, Yaro remembered, renovations were done in the park and it was renamed Parc Urbain Bangr-Weoogo, meaning 'the urban park of the forest of knowledge'. Even though he had said his morning prayer at home, he bowed his head and said another silent one. Today was a big day for him. Teaching at the university had been a dream of his for years.

Founded in 1974, the University of Ouagadougou was located in the area of Zogona. It was almost an hour's ride from Yaro's home on his bicycle. The building on the campus that housed the Academic Department and Program was relatively new. This is where he would begin his career at the university. He would be teaching educational strategies, learned at Northern Arizona University, to prospective teachers. As he walked into the building, he straightened his new suit (one of the three he had purchased in Flagstaff), and hurried toward his office and new position.

* * * * *

"Yaro, let's not have any more children." Anzounou was always direct so it should not have surprised him that there had been no hint during these past six months of her desire to stop with Ana.

Yaro was surprised, but he didn't show it. "Ah, how so? Tell me about this, my beautiful one. Why do you suggest this?" More children had been their plan. As he waited for her answer, he couldn't help but wonder if it was somehow his fault. His wife was no fool, and maybe it was only because custom didn't allow for intimate sharing of feelings, that Anzounou had held her tongue. Had she discerned that his heart belonged to someone in America? Could such a knowing exist in a relationship that was comfortable, kind, and peaceful?

"I thought first of this when you were in America, but since your return I am thinking of it more. There are several reasons, my husband, and it is time for me to make them known to you." It was obvious that she was unsure of his reaction, but she continued. "You will be leaving again in a few years to get your PhD, and I don't want the responsibility of more children while you are away. Too, we will always have the financial commitment to your family and that will take from our monies. You know that I don't have a problem with that, and I am willing to contribute money by

77

teaching until my old age. Also, I want Ana to have the best and highest education possible, and that will mean leaving Burkina Faso. She is so beautiful and smart, like you, that I want her to have the advantage of international travel and schooling. We can't possibly provide this for several children." Anzounou smiled and added with more volume and confidence in her voice. "It is not just about children either. I want a lovely home with more rooms and modernization. There is enough space on our property to add a master bedroom and bath, like you told me people have in Flagstaff. Ana could then have our room instead of sleeping on the couch, and too the kitchen needs remodeling. But, new furniture and rugs are all the company room needs to be very nice."

"Ah, for sure, I should not have brought you all those American Home magazines," Yaro laughed and pulled her to him for assurance that she need not be hesitant to speak her mind. "Now tell me about you," he encouraged. "Money for my family; an expensive education for our brilliant one; a beautiful home for all three of us, and for you? What is it you want, Anzounou?"

Tears came to her eyes as she realized that he was not mad at her nor was he mocking her. She laid her head on his chest and softly continued. "I too want to experience other countries. I would not want to go to the United States or South America, but Europe instead. I have been reading about teaching in foreign countries and when Ana is ready to leave for her university studies, if I could get a teaching job in France that would be wonderful." She sighed and added even more quietly, "I am thinking that it would be most fair if both of us were able to have a large life."

Yaro held her close and tears came to his eyes. "For sure, my dear one, we can change the vision of our life together to include your dreams. Let me suggest that during the years before Ana is ready to leave for the university, that you get a second teaching endorsement in another field of study. That way, when the time is right, you will be most qualified to get a teaching position in France."

Her squeal of excitement was not like her at all. She fairly bounded out of his arms and started dancing around the room chanting, "Allah be praised for such a loving husband".

Yaro was so relieved. She didn't know. She wasn't disappointed in his crippled way of loving her. "Yes, Allah be praised," he said too, but not for the same reason.

It was play time for Ana, but not for her parents. She would gather her papers, colors, and readers for another evening of 'school'; Anzounou did her assignments for the night courses she was taking at the university to become a certified math teacher, and Yaro was hitting the books again in preparation for the scholarship exams he must pass for his PhD program. It was a family affair and a nightly routine now at their kitchen table. That was the way of it, routine. One year passed, and then it was two. They studied together night after night in a house that was always in some stage of improvement. They were the three musketeers! Ana was very advanced for her first year in school; however, she didn't have the same purpose Yaro had had when he was only six. Ana didn't have to save her family; she only had to save herself. Money was being put aside monthly for her higher education and as a first grader she had already decided that she would go to Paris to study architecture. Anzounou was sure that their home being under a constant state of remodeling had influenced her.

Yaro was the most popular of all the education professors at the university. His classes were very challenging because he demanded the highest standards from his students. Nevertheless, they were always filled because he had the reputation of sharing his experience in Flagstaff with his classes. His tales of the wild west in Arizona were famous. He motivated his students with descriptions of the American life-style and advanced culture. However, he didn't neglect to share his personal experience at the hands of white people. His lack of bitterness was a puzzle, no doubt, because his students had no way of knowing how his experience with Leisa had changed his life there at NAU. Actually, telling his stories about the United States was a way of keeping her in his mind. So instead of hiding his memories, he could talk about the people he had met via her; he could describe Lake Powell, Sedona, the Grand Canyon, and he could talk about the homes and the parties he attended during those last months in Flagstaff. The fact that her presence in his tales was never acknowledged, was of no consequence. His students benefited from his stories, and he did too. Leisa remained alive to him even though he had not spoken to her in years.

They lived so easily together that Anzounou seldom let her imagination wander to what they didn't have. He was the most considerate of husbands, and she realized that not many men would have agreed to her dream. Therefore, it wasn't often that she let herself entertain the unacknowledged reality. Yaro could not be faulted as a father, provider, or companion, but he was not her lover. Sex, like everything else in their life, was friendly. It was the same way, at the same time, and for the same reason every week. Actually, to be perfectly honest, it was not all that different from the way it had been from the very first of their marriage. Yet since his return from America, on some level she sensed his emotional absence more than ever. He was a considerate lover, but not a personal one. She always ended these bouts of pondering by scolding herself for her quandary. All her lady friends at school were jealous of her. She had a husband who did not insist on many children; he was allowing her to study at the university, and she had his approval to plan towards a teaching career in a foreign country. All that, plus providing a home that was the envy of the neighborhood. Certainly she was happy, she told herself. Not to be, would be a blaspheme against Allah.

* * * * *

"If I was not planning to be in France one day, I could not bear this." Anzounou was helping Yaro pack with tears streaming down her face. "Of all places to be accepted - France".

He too was near tears. His hard work had paid off once more. Because of his high scores he had won a full scholarship to the University of Nantes to complete his many years of education with a PhD in Educational Leadership. It would take him three years to earn his doctorate. He had to rush with it because there would only be Anzounou's salary to support his family while he was away. No more construction on the house, for sure, and no money to his parents while he was gone. And, only a small amount each month towards Ana's college fund, but Anzounou would continue with her math certification. Her future could not be suspended for his.

"Now Ana, you are old enough to know that I must leave you and Mama, but I will be coming back when I finish my schooling. You know about schooling, don't you? You know how we all have to go to school so we can fulfill our destiny? So, you won't be upset with me this time?" Yaro's memories of how long it took for Ana to welcome him back into her life were still hurtful.

"Oh, for sure Papa. I understand and it is okay now. I am a big girl this time, and I will be going to school just like Mama," Ana was not crying or upset, and it made Yaro chuckle to hear her use his habitual phrase.

"I will not be so far away this time, dear one, so if there should be some trouble, I can come home." Yaro assured his wife.

Anzounou smiled at him. "You don't worry yourself about us. I am capable of anything needed, and we will talk on the phone once a week like before. I will be excited to hear all about Nantes because one day I will be going to France." She laughed, "I too have a destiny."

Getting the scholarship to the University of Nantes in France, instead of some school in the United States, was initially painful for Yaro. Had he been returning to America, Leisa would once again be in his life. There was no way he could be in the same country as she and not contact her. But since they could not yet put their lives together, Allah had provided a way around temptation. When the time was right, all he would have to do is call Leisa's daughter. Never was there any doubt that it would be too late or impossible. His only challenge was to be patient and trusting of 'Divine Order'. And being so busy with his advanced studies would help.

The University of Nantes is a well-known French university, with approximately 30,000 students, of which the vast majority is French. It is the second largest university in France. The current university was founded in 1970 under the terms of the 1968 law which reformed French higher education. This newly established institution replaced the former University of Nantes which had been founded in the early 1960s. This itself was a re-establishment of the original University of Nantes which was established by papal bull in 1460 but was abolished during the French Revolution.

As Yaro walked around the campus, he was greeted by strangers who had no visible reaction to the color of his skin. Unlike America, black didn't register with them as separate or inferior. Yes, he thought to himself, these years are going to be so much kinder. For one thing, he didn't have an eighteen year old roommate. Instead, he was privileged to have a very small dorm room to himself. This was the usual accommodation for the older, foreign students.

Ah, and the city! What a place of wonder. Nantes was historically part of Brittany, but now is the capital of the Pays de la Loire region of northwestern France. It is located on the Loire River, and with almost ¾ of a million people, it is the sixth largest city in France. It is considered one of the most desirable places to live in France, especially for young professionals who enjoy the arts and don't want to live in Paris. There is inexpensive public transportation, so unlike Flagstaff, Arizona, Yaro could go anywhere in the city to sightsee. Whenever his studies allowed, he would take the time to visit the many tourist attractions and report to Anzounou weekly. He didn't rush his visits to the area attractions because, unlike tourists, he had three years there to see everything. He did mail Anzounou brochures of the places he would see and then after his visit, he would talk to her on the phone about it. He could tell that it was her main interest in their weekly conversation. Once he had quickly reported on his health and the progress of his classes, he would spend the rest of the time describing some famous place. There was Nantes Cathedral Saints Peter and Paul, begun in 1434. It is a Gothic cathedral with a 11th century crypt that is a museum of religions. And Yaro really enjoyed the museum and the native house of Jules Verne, and he would go back time and again to the Musee des Beaux-arts, a highly celebrated fine arts museum built around an airy courtyard that featured works ranging from the Italian Primitives to contemporary artists. Yes, Nantes was nothing like Flagstaff. Both were spectacular, but could not be compared. For sure, he was much happier in France. However, there was no Leisa. There were many beautiful women who turned his head, but there was no one to love. His heart belonged to a tall, blond beauty whom he hadn't seen in over two years.

The small sidewalk cafes were his favorite places to

spend a weekend afternoon with some book that needed reading. The owners were friendly and were happy to have him sit at one of their tables for hours without ordering anything more than tea. They did try to persuade him to drink their famous local wines, such as Muscadet and Gros Plant, or to eat the fromage du cure nantais (a cow's milk cheese developed by a priest near Nantes). Yaro didn't have the money to eat anything there, and drinking wine was not allowed, so until he became acquainted with the other regulars, he only purchased one cup of tea. Thank goodness it was refilled as needed. But people were so friendly to him that as the months passed it became their habit to invite him to join them at their table for food, or to invite him to dinner parties in their homes. Like in Flagstaff, after Leisa became a part of his life, he entertained them by telling his new friends about his culture and way of life in Burkina Faso. Yes, the three years in France passed much more quickly and happily than did the two in the United States. Unlike his stay on the campus of NAU in Flagstaff, he created a life for himself in Nantes. He joined university organizations, and he had a circle of friends in the city as well. He had proven Leisa correct when she had suggested to him that one's experience in the world is in direct relation to their emotional and spiritual selves. Clearly, Yaro was in a healthy space, psychologically. With every passing year, he was becoming more and more a leader of men, and he would tell you that that was his destiny.

CHAPTER SEVEN

"Papa, Papa, Papa," screamed Ana as she ran ahead of her mother into Yaro's arms. Anzounou approached smiling, but allowed them their seconds together before she joined her daughter in his arms.

"Welcome home, my husband." He had known that those would be the first words out of her mouth. Anzounou was as beautiful as ever, he noticed immediately. No years showed on her face, and her body was still that of a girl's.

"Ah, my dear, dear ones! I am back – back to my treasures. Allah be praised." Yaro's tears of happiness joined theirs as they stayed locked in each other's arms.

How heartfelt it was to see his home again. He went immediately to the warm, cheerful kitchen that was painted a sunshine yellow where many a 'school' hour had been spent around the white table in the middle of the room. Nothing had changed anywhere in the house, and that was to his liking. Ana's small bedroom was filled with the essence of an eight year old whose preference for pink was obvious. The master bedroom (that Anzounou had insisted on and designed) was a welcoming place of jade walls and native wood. The wood framed double bed was so inviting with its dusty burgundy bedspread fabric and a variety of decorator pillows in various patterns that matched the curtains on the two windows. Being a home economics teacher, his wife knew how to sew the curtains, bedspread, and pillow covers. She had put much thought into the look she wanted and many hours making all that was needed to create a room that was soft, yet not feminine. What a difference from my cell of a dorm room, thought Yaro, as he absorbed the ambience of the bedroom. How rewarding it was to be home with his family. And such a beautiful home it was, thanks to Anzounou's dream and her hard work.

Because she remembered the steady stream of visitors who came uninvited the last time Yaro returned to Burkina Faso, Anzounou was prepared to avoid that immediate interruption to his homecoming today. She had a special family dinner planned for the three of them, and to insure that they would not be delayed in their private time together, she had arranged for an open-house the following afternoon. "All your colleagues from the university, even your parents and all our friends and neighbors will come tomorrow to celebrate your accomplishment and welcome you home," Anzounou explained as she led him to the table and chairs outside under the tree in the back yard. "Sit now and wait for Ana to bring you your tea. It has been her plan to serve you, and she is making it special with a small cake she baked for you."

"Ah, for sure. What a blessed difference from my last homecoming. Remember how she hid in your skirts and it took weeks before she would let me into her little world?" Yaro sat down wearily into one of the bambo chairs they had gotten as a wedding gift nine years ago. He was tired, but as he waited to be served by his only child, he held his wife's hand and sighed deeply. "Allah has surely blessed us. My heart is full of rejoicing and gratitude." Yet, as he complimented his eight year old daughter on the delicious cake and tea, Leisa came from his heart into his mind. He could not anticipate how she would ever be a part of his life. And, thank goodness that was not his job, he reminded himself. Allah was in charge of that, as He was all other aspects of his life. He would do his part by praising Him and appreciating all his good fortune. Somehow, it would be.

This time, following his return with his PhD in Educational Leadership, Yaro had a position waiting for him at the Burkina Faso Ministry of Education. He did purchase a motorbike for the daily trip to the government building, but it wasn't long before he realized that he would be traveling throughout his country as much as to his office there in the capitol city.

Yaro was now responsible for guiding and advising all those students who were candidates for higher education. He would travel by rail to the major cities: Banfora, Tenkodogo, Dori, Djibo, Yako, Diapaga, Koudougou, and others to meet with students to offer all the possibilities for university level education. Additionally, he would help those students who were planning to study abroad. As the months went by, he became very well known and appreciated for his expertise and willingness to assist students fulfill their destinies. It was a good life, a busy one, and a purposeful one.

The letter came to his office. It had taken three weeks to arrive from New York. Anytime Yaro was tempted to think that his country was making progress in modern communication, all he had to do was notice how unreliable the mail service was. It was a miracle that it got there at all. He had just returned from one of his week long business trips, and the in-basket on his desk was full of correspondence from within the department. But he noticed it immediately. It was the high quality paper of the envelope that got his attention. Did the return address really read, UNESCO, United Nations, New York, NY?

How he managed to remain at work and concentrate on his many tasks, he would never know. After reading the letter, he had returned it to the envelope and placed it in his briefcase in a state of shock. There was so much work to do, that he had to force himself to put it from his mind until he got home. The secretary's lips were moving, but what was she saying? His heart was pounding in his ears and his throat was tightening up. "Allah, Allah," he prayed silently. "Help me remain calm."

"Come sit down, Anzounou, this letter will explain. I will read it to you. You too, Ana, if you wish. This is the most important letter Papa has ever gotten." Both his wife and daughter were breathless with anticipation, and Yaro's voice revealed how incredulous he was to be reading the words.

"Dear Dr. Yaro Bomou,
The UNESCO (United Nations Educational, Scientific, Cultural Organization) is apprised of your outstanding abilities in the service of your country's ministry of education. Consequently, it is the purpose of this correspondence

to acquaint you with our agency, and to invite you to consider joining our staff here in New York City at the United Nations Headquarters.

UNESCO promotes quality education systems at the post-primary levels by assisting policy-makers, curriculum developers, trainers and teachers to reform national education systems. Its objective is to create more learning opportunities for young people and adults and to make national programs more relevant to science and technology-led societies and labor market needs while being consistent with sustainable development. UNESCO advocates education strategies that are gender-inclusive; increasing girls' access to secondary, technical and vocational education and training and encouraging them to pursue interests in the fields of science and technology are considered crucial.

For learners who are outside the formal school system and other special groups like disadvantaged youth, UNESCO advocates flexible secondary-level learning opportunities that impart the knowledge and skills, both social and practical, to enable these learners to engage in productive livelihoods as responsible citizens in their particular cultural, economic and technological contexts.

In order to translate innovative ideas into concrete action, UNESCO promotes policy dialogue and supports capacity building by organizing seminars and workshops for policy and decision-makers; strengthening networking and partnership among key stakeholders, and conducting research into the emerging trends and challenges for education at the national, regional and international levels.

As you know, Burkina Faso joined UNESCO in 1960, and is one of the 35 countries implementing its Literacy Initiative for Empowerment (LIFE), a ten-year initiative aimed at achieving the goals of the United Nations Literacy Decade (2003-2012). Your country also participates in the UNESCO Teacher Training Initiative for sub-Saharan Africa which will assist the continent's 46 sub-Saharan countries in restructuring national teacher policies and teacher educa-tion.

You come highly recommended to us, and if you are interested in joining our staff here in New York, please fax us your resume, three letters of recommendation, copies of your transcripts from both Northern Arizona University and Nantes University, and a letter of interest. There is currently more than one position you are highly qualified for, if our general information about you is correct. Additionally, an immediate email acknowledging the receipt of this letter would be appreciated.

Sincerely,
Dr. Thomas Cunningham, Human Resources Director"

Anzounou was speechless, but Ana started dancing around the room chanting, "We are going to America, to America, to America."

Yaro dropped the letter onto the kitchen table and

took his wife's hands and lifted her to her feet. Her black eyes filled her face. "Is Ana right? Is this for all three of us, or will you go alone?" Anzounou was cautious with her enthusiasm.

"I have no idea. I must ask. There are so many un-knowns that I am dizzy with questions. Will I work only in New York, or will I be sent to the many African countries to help implement the UNESCO programs? Might I be in different African countries as much as in New York? Is housing provided for UN staff, and if so, is family included? But, even without knowing anything about what the position requires, is this not the most unexpected and amazing possibility for my career?" Yaro hugged his silent wife and then turned to step to the kitchen sink. He bent with emotion. Back in Leisa's country! He couldn't get his breath and as he slumped forward Anzounou was instantly there to hold him.

"Come, let me help you to the bed", she advised. "And Ana, don't be alarmed. Nothing is wrong with Papa. He is just so excited that it has made him very tired. Help me get him to the bedroom."

He slept not one wink all night. Between his heart and his mind he got no peace. Would his wife consider his behavior over-reacting to the news of this job? How was it possible that she could be there beside him in their bed and not feel his thoughts of Leisa? "Leisa, my Diarabi" he softly cried into his pillow. Memories would not be denied. He saw her smile a greeting at him when he walked into her office; he heard her introduce a theory on human behavior in her customary way, '..... It has been my experience.....' and

92

he felt her hunger for his body while never tempting him to commit adultery. As the night hours passed he was tormented with the realization that geography was the only way he and Leisa would actually be any closer. If his family went with him, Leisa would not be in his life. If they didn't go, that still didn't put Leisa into his life. He would still be a married man. By the time the sun came up, he was sitting outside with his habitual cup of tea, and reluctantly he admitted to himself that it was not time for the phone call to Leisa's daughter. He was very weary as he said his morning prayers. Nevertheless, he was extravagant with his praise to Allah for the career possibility, and emotional with his supplications for patience and understanding. He came close to reminding Allah that Leisa was his destiny, but he stopped short of that irreverence.

The answers to his many questions were quick in coming. Thank goodness, email and fax communication was no respecter of countries. Even the interview between a committee there in New York and himself was via speaker phone. The decision by the UNESCO Human Resources Hiring Team was that Yaro was needed in New York. He would work in the International Bureau of Education (a department in UNESCO) because of his educational emphasis and experience in curriculum development. Yaro listened intently to the explanation of IBE. The voice on the phone explained that it works to strengthen the competencies for the management of curriculum development among decision makers, specialist, researchers and practitioners at international, regional and national levels. All the activities are orientated towards capacity building and include:

organizing training activities and providing technical advice to strengthen capacities in critical areas of curriculum design, planning and renewal; facilitating regional networking and exchange among experts from national curriculum departments; promoting action-research activities addressing curriculum development in post-conflict and transition countries; developing modules, training tools and resource materials in curriculum policy-making and development, and working towards the constitution of a Global Curriculum Network representing a worldwide community of practitioners devoted to curriculum development.

And although IBE also provides advisory services to UNESCO member countries, Yaro was assured that this would not require him to travel. The IBE's Resource Bank provides the relevant and timely data on a wide range of educational issues that he would use to help him customize the appropriate curriculum needed in each country.

Three months' time was offered to get his affairs settled and move to New York. And yes, his family was welcome to come with him. A one-way flight would be provided for the three of them, and assistance given with finding housing there. They were told that many of the full-time employees purchased real estate in New Jersey, and then commuted to work on the train. Yaro especially liked this idea because he had never learned to drive a car, and he sure didn't want to learn how on the east coast of the United States. He might live in Africa, but he did know the reputation of city driving in New York.

"You should have been studying English instead of mathematics all these years," teased Yaro as they lingered under their backyard tree before bedtime. "Now, Ana here has inherited my gift for languages, so she can help you with the grocery shopping." Father and daughter chuckled at the prospect, while Anzounou just pretended to pout.

"Groceries are the least of my worries. How about not being able to read street signs, newspapers, or understand the television programs? Thank goodness I have three months to take a crash course in English. And you there, the one who can speak English – you must make it a habit to talk to me now in English – not make fun of my ignorance," she laughed with them. "Seriously though, I am going to sign up for that conversational English course at the university. I won't be here long enough to finish it, but anything I learn will help." Anzounou's light mood changed to one of genuine concern and the question that had been haunting her spilled out, "Oh Yaro, this is all so wonderful for you and Ana, but what in the world am I going to do in America? I can't teach there because I don't speak English."

"For sure, you will go on with your life too. There will be a way for you to continue a conversational English course, and while you are doing this you will be more available to Ana because she is going to need your help getting adjusted to school this in new country. You know how busy you will be furnishing our home, and then when you are proficient in English and you have completed the last two math courses you need to become a certified teacher, you will work again. You have never been stopped from accomplishing whatever you wanted - why would that change now?'

Her husband's confidence lifted her mood. It was

going to be a giant learning curve for her, but at least she would not be doing it alone. She would be with her family, and Yaro would be so much help to her because he already knew English. Good grief, be more grateful and less afraid, she told herself. At least she won't have the kind of experience her husband had at Northern Arizona University with people not being welcoming. And for goodness sakes, her husband's position with the United Nations will put her in the company of people from all over the world. Too, Yaro had assured her that the Americans they would come to know, who lived in the cosmopolitan area of New York, were less influenced by race.

It felt good to Yaro for this to be a family leaving, not just him going away for a few years as in the past. Always before, his excitement to be starting a new life in some other country had been tempered with sadness at leaving the ones he loved. Not so these days. The only remorse was around not seeing his parents maybe ever again. They were getting old and travel was very foreign to them. In fact, them coming to his home for the open-house Anzounou planned when he returned from France was the only time they had ever come to the city to see him. The good thing in all this, he reminded himself, was that he would be able to send even more money than ever before. After all, financial support for his parents and siblings had been the motivation years ago when he was the one selected to be educated. Too, his parents were living among all their other children and grandchildren, thus they would be well cared for until they died. No need for regret concerning his parents. He had brothers and sisters, but they weren't familiar people to him.

It would be a happy life in America. With his child and wife, he would have his family with him.

And about Leisa? There were no answers. As he made plans to sell his home; give furniture away; decide on what he treasured enough to transport to New York – he prayed. He prayed like never before in his life, and his 5-times-a-day prayers were a mixture of thanksgiving and pleading. He didn't trust himself to not contact her. Would knowing that he had nothing to offer her, be enough to keep him from picking up the phone and calling her daughter?

* * * * *

"You aren't asleep are you?" she asked.

"No I'm not, but why aren't you?" Yaro mumbled from his side of the bed.

Very softly and slowly she released these words into the darkness. "I'm not going. I'm not going to New York with you."

It took several seconds before he finally whispered, "Anzounou, what are you saying?"

She had been right. The tone of his voice and the energy coming from his immobile body told her that, yes, he was shocked, but not horrified.

"I have been wrong....all these years. Now I must admit that I cannot live my life with a husband who is not in love with me, nor me with him. You honor me, you provide for me, and you are kind and loving, but you have no passion for me. Me!! This is true, is it not?" she finished with a breath of resoluteness.

He didn't even consider hesitating or hedging. "It is

97

true", he breathed.

"Neither of us have ever been in love with the other. True?" she asked.

"When we married, I didn't know that being in love was a requirement for true happiness."

"But now you do?"

Yaro sighed and began his confession with these words, "Yes, now I do."

Anzounou waited for him to begin his story. As a way to signal her encouragement and lack of blame, she reached for his hand.

"It was during the last two months of my time in Flagstaff that I came to know what passion for another is all about. Her name is Leisa, and she worked in the education department where I attended classes. She saved my life. By then, I was so miserably alone and friendless that I was sick. Her invitations into her private life and the society she introduced me to, propelled me from the brink of suicide to a restoration of myself as an acknowledged human being."

Yaro could hear her slow, deep breathing, but she made no move to speak.

He continued, "For sure, it was more than that. I cannot explain why I fell in love with her, but I did. It has been about five years ago now, and even though we were never intimate and I have not corresponded with her in any way, I feel that she is the only person in this world for me. It makes no sense, and it pains me to tell you this, but I suspect that you already know."

"No, not really. I was only certain that you have no passion for me."

Quietly he ventured, "And that is also true for you? You aren't in love with me either?" Was it relief he was feeling? Could she hear it in his question?

"I don't honestly think I knew to expect anything more than what we had together from the very beginning of our marriage," she began. "What I felt for you was warm and comforting; not fire and desire. And, our lives fit so perfectly. You know we have never been disagreeable with each other. There is a kind and loving atmosphere in our home, and we have both worked together for the futures we want for ourselves. Actually, your career has developed beyond my wildest dreams, and I have good reason to think that mine will too, in time. No, I have no tangible reason to be living a life that feels unfulfilled. Nevertheless, it turns out that I am."

Yaro moved to turn on the bedside light. She had sat up now, and was looking at him with the faintest of smiles on her beautiful face.

"Full disclosure makes for real intimacy, don't you agree?" she said as she got out of bed. "I'll make us some tea."

Yaro followed her into the kitchen and sat in silence until she served the tea, and joined him at their familiar table. He had never seen her more radiant and vibrant. She was actually smiling as she said, "You must be the one to file for a divorce. A Moslem woman getting a divorce would be too complicated and time consuming."

"Do you have a plan? I get the feeling that this conversation is coming at the end, rather than at the beginning of this major life change." His heart was accepting of what was happening, but his mind was incredulous.

"I want to move to France. I can complete my teaching certification in math at the university you attended, and then Ana can also go to school there when she is older. I already love Nantes and it has been a secret dream of mine to live there. Do you remember all those brochures you mailed me, and your descriptions of how much you enjoyed your years there when you were getting your PhD?"

"For sure, I remember. And yes, it is a wonderful city. We will sell this house and the money will be for your life there. Too, I will send you a good amount from my salary each month."

Judging from her demeanor, Anzounou could have been closing an ordinary financial deal…not a marriage. "Okay, but what about your parents and siblings? Your responsibility to your family must not change."

Yaro smiled at her as he assured her that it would not. How was it possible, he wondered, that they were sitting casually at their kitchen table making plans to end their marriage? And how could they both be feeling such a sense of well being about divorce? And what was Allah's role in all this, if any? Yaro had no answers, but her shining eyes and his leaping heart were all the evidence needed to know that they were doing the right thing.

CHAPTER EIGHT

"Mom, who is Yaro Bomou?" It was her daughter calling from the ranch.

Her heart stopped! "Who?" was the only word that would come out of Leisa's mouth. She had clearly heard his name, but she couldn't believe her ears.

"Mom, a man with some sort of foreign accent called just a few minutes ago and asked for your phone number. I wrote down his name, it is spelled y-a-r-o-b-o-m-o-u. I may not be pronouncing it correctly. I hope it was alright to give it to him, because he also wanted your mailing address, and I gave that to him too. Did I do the wrong thing?"

Leisa spent the time it took her daughter, Claire, to tell her about the phone call to try to calm herself and regroup. "Oh, yes, yes, that's fine. He is a friend from years ago when I worked at Northern Arizona University. I'm just surprised because I haven't heard from him in ages. Did he say when he would call me?"

"Yes, he asked me to tell you that he will call you tomorrow morning at 9 AM your time. What did he mean by 'your time'?"

"He lives in Africa, so there is a time difference to consider. Did he say anything else?" Leisa knew that she didn't sound like herself, and there would be no fooling

Claire. Her only daughter could always sniff her out when something was wrong.

"No Mom, but I have some questions. You sound a little off center. Do you have time to talk?"

"Not now, Sweetie, I'm expecting Kitty this morning and I need to get dressed." Leisa lied. "We are going shopping, so I'll call you tomorrow. We will have more to talk about then."

She couldn't keep back the tears another minute. As she hung up the phone she could feel her heart pounding and she was sure she couldn't stand, so she didn't try. As she sat in her wicker chair on the patio this beautiful summer morning, she couldn't think. Several minutes passed before she could do anything but cry. Then, just like a lightening bolt had struck her, she jumped up and started squealing,"Oh God, God, Oh God!"

Her across-the-walk neighbor heard her and came rushing out onto her patio with concern written all over her face.

When Leisa saw her, she realized that she was causing a commotion, so she motioned to her. "I'm okay. Nothing is wrong. In fact, everything is perfect! I just got the most welcomed phone call of my life. I'm sorry if I scared you." Leisa danced over towards the neighbor's patio and just beamed, "I don't act like anything is wrong, now do I?" She gave the curious lady a quick hug before dancing, and twirling her way back onto her own patio. Picking up her coffee cup, Leisa opened the screen door to go inside. She must not disturb the neighborhood any further.

Once inside her apartment, she threw herself onto the

bed and the tears came again. She felt hot and cold at the same time. Actually, she was dizzy and breathless. Hugging her pillow and rolling with the fervor of her joy, she didn't try to think. She just wanted to drown in the emotion of it all. As the minutes passed, her exhaustion quieted her and she became still, eventually regaining enough composure to walk into the bathroom and wash her face.

Then she went into the living room and just stood there still as a stone, and tried to survive the bombardment of questions that came at her. Where was he? What about his family? It has been five years. Does he still love me? Then her memories took over. Yaro's words came back to her as though he had spoken them yesterday. "I won't call you until the time is right." She remembered him saying, "You are my destiny. We must trust that we will be together again, some day…..some how."

It was Sunday and she was sitting by the phone. Thank God she had had time to prepare for his call. Since yesterday Yaro had not been out of her mind for a minute. Everything she did was flavored with his presence: grocery shopping, getting the car washed, going to Barnes and Nobles Booksellers to pick up a book she had ordered, and going to the park to jog in the late afternoon. It was a solitary day. There was no way she could talk to or be around any of her friends. Anyone who knew her would notice instantly that something was up, so she declined every invitation to join others for anything.

Nothing worked. She couldn't concentrate on her new book more than a paragraph or two, so she put it down and went to the pool after dark. No one was there, (it was

Saturday night and only folks without a life went to swim on party night), therefore she was not interrupted as she floated on her back, looking up at the stars, and remembering those two months together five years ago. TV couldn't hold her attention either, so around ten o'clock she took a Tylenol PM to help her escape into blessed sleep.

"Diarabi? Is that you?" His voice was the same – low, strong, gentle, assured, and his term of endearment remembered.

It took her a second to get a sound to come out of her mouth. "Yes, it's me," was all she could manage. In the silence she could hear him breathing, and it helped to loosen her tongue. "Oh Yaro, my God, it's you. After all these years, you are calling me."

"For sure, my Diarabi, I told you I would when the time was right, and it is."

"Oh my God, what does that mean," she interrupted. "What has happened?"

"You must not require the answers today, Diarabi. Let us please just make some plans and our talk be about you and your life. I have much to tell you, but it must keep until we meet in New York City. I am hoping you can join me in July for a week's visit. Can you come? Are you married or ill or anything that would keep you from me?" His voice was charged with emotion and longing.

"New York City?" She was sure she sounded stupid, but it was just all too overwhelming for her to be her usual 'together' self. "Why New York City? Are you moving there? Are you still married? I'm sorry, Yaro, but why can't you tell me anything?" She hated the way she was almost whimpering.

"Please just tell me you can come. I will tell you everything that has happened to me since we parted, but only in your company. I will not talk about my life over the phone. Diarabi, I am not trying to be mysterious, I just can't explain anything now. I cannot talk about me now. Will you accept that? Will you come?"

"Yes, yes – a million times yes. When and where is all I need to know." Answers could wait because nothing mattered enough to keep her from seeing him this summer.

"Ah, I can be happy now. You will come. Good, I can tell you the date, but if you will, for me, please decide on the hotel and make the arrangements. It will be most difficult to do that from here because I am in Burkina Faso. The date is July 10th to the 17th. We will need a room from the night of the10th through 16th." He sounded like an executive accustomed to giving directives.

"Wait just a minute, let me get something to write on. I don't trust my memory," she interrupted. "....Okay, I'm back and you said you want a room for the nights of July 10th through and 16th? And does the hotel need to be in any certain part of the city? And what price are you willing to pay? I understand that they can be very expensive."

"Those dates are correct, and I have a living allowance of 500 dollars a day for this one week. So, I would think that anything 300 or under for a hotel room would be good, and the location can be within walking distance of Central Park. Now, if that is all the information you need to know, I want to hear about you. We have only a few minutes to talk, but will you tell me about your life?" His administrative tone was gone and replaced in the last two sentences with his lover's voice.

"Well," laughed Leisa, "In a few words or less, I live in Houston, TX in my own rented apartment. I have just taken an early retirement from teaching in a public high school, and my plan is to begin working on a PhD in Transpersonal Psychology in the fall. As you have guessed by my accepting your invitation, I am not married or involved with anyone. Not that I haven't had my chances," she teased, "but I've been waiting for this man who told me five years ago that I was his destiny. Can you imagine such a thing," she laughed. Clearly, she was becoming more relaxed with the fact that she was actually talking to Yaro.

"Ah, for sure! Sounds like a smart fellow to me and one who knows about these things. You know, the things of the heart," Yaro too was now getting into a lighter mood. "So tell me now, Diarabi, you have kept my promise in your heart? You knew I would come for you?" His voice was making love to her, and it was almost as effective as if he had her in his arms.

"I have to confess that the word 'knew' is a little too strong. I mainly went by evidence. You see, of the men I have dated, none of them were 'home' like you are to me. You and I only had those couple of months together, but time hasn't been a major factor in our relationship, has it? It has been five years without any communication and it looks like that hasn't changed anything either." Leisa felt like she was melting into the phone. "Oh, next month – I will finally get to be with you again. Oh God, I can hardly stand it." She finished in a husky whisper.

106

Yaro ignored her comment and to her chagrin she noticed that his business voice was back: the topic of conversation changed and he was rushed. "We will meet at the hotel of your choice. My plane is in at 4 PM so I will call you. This is your cell phone number, isn't it? I'll get a taxi and be to the hotel as soon as possible."

"Yes, this is my cell phone number. I'll get in earlier and be waiting for you. Oh, I can't believe any of this, I just can't." Tears were coming and her voice was cracking. He could be Mr. Composure if he needed to, but she wasn't going to fake it.

"Diarabi, I will not talk to you again until I land in New York, but I want you to watch the mail. I am sending you a letter. It will help you understand my feelings, those not expressed now over the phone. I must go. You see, I am in a semi-public place, so please understand my tone and words. The letter, it will encourage you."

His letter came ten days later.

"My dearest Diarabi,

Remember the first time we were together, and you drove me to Sedona for the picnic on Bell Rock? That was when I first knew that destiny had determined that we were to find each other. It was a knowing with my heart because all in my mind contradicted that truth. Now, at long last, my mind can join my heart, so I come to you. Destiny is now putting our lives together, as our hearts have always been.

I will never leave you again. Please accept, with patience, that I cannot, in this letter, explain the facts of how this is,

*but just know that all has now been made possible for our
life together.*

I am coming.

*First, last, and always yours,
Yaro"*

* * * * *

Like Yaro, Leisa couldn't explain to Claire over the
phone, so the following weekend she drove to the ranch to
give a full report. Not to her entire family – no, only Claire.
She had some hope that Claire would be accepting of this
new development in her life, but she sure wasn't certain of
anyone else: Kitty, her brother, or her son or any of her life-
long friends. "For sure, Shotsy," Leisa loved to use Yaro's
habitual phrase. She was only a few miles from the ranch
and she had talked to her car the entire trip. "Yes, for sure.
I'll start with Claire because her reaction will give me an
idea of what to expect from the others." Leisa laughed as
she patted Shotsy on her dash. "No doubt you will be glad to
be rid of me when we get to the ranch. Please understand, I
just had to practice my story and you were the perfect one to
listen, because, of course, you never say a word back." She
laughed as she tried to remember if Yaro knew she talked to
her car.

"Okay, Mom, what's up?"

Claire had gotten rid of everyone because she knew
they needed privacy. It was late afternoon and no longer so
hot, therefore her husband had taken the two sunshine girls

fishing and no one else was expected for at least two hours. "Something major is in the wind. I know you too well. Tell me, am I to be the first to know?"

"As always, Daughter-Mine. Why would I change my habits at this late date? If memory serves me correctly, you were the first to know that your dad and I were getting a divorce."

"Mom, really! I knew years before you told me. You could cut the tension with a knife at the house, and I felt it. You certainly weren't fooling me with your 'everything is fine' persona. So tell me what's up now, then I'll tell you how long I have known." Claire grinned and settled into the big, comfy couch in the living room with her glass of wine.

Leisa smiled, "Your on! And the bottom line is, I'm going to New York City on July 10th to meet a man from Africa that I have been in love with for five years."

"Africa? You are in love with a man from Africa?" Claire was not smiling. "Mom, this means he is black, right?"

"He sure is. Probably blacker than any man you have ever seen. He was a graduate student at NAU when I was working there. We had some classes together, that's how we met." Leisa sounded like she was talking about just anyone, and that wasn't what she wanted to convey.

It was clear that Claire hadn't anticipated this kind of news. Clearly, she was stunned, so for what felt like an eternity, she sat silently and looked at her mother. Finally, she said, "Actually, I am more surprised by the 'I'm in love with' part than the 'black' part. Mom, I don't think I have ever heard you say you were IN LOVE with anyone. You say 'I love him' but never, 'I am IN LOVE'. Right?"

Leisa smiled and took a sip of wine. "You hit the nail on the head, Claire. I was in love with your dad many years ago, but you're right - no one since. Do you realize that I haven't seen or talked to Yaro in five years, and I still know that without a doubt, I am in love with him. He calls it destiny." She could see the skepticism in Claire's eyes at the mention of 'destiny', so she hurriedly added. "Personally, I can't testify to what destiny or fate has to do with anything, but I can assure you that this is the man for me. If he wants to think of it as destiny that is fine with me, and whether I do or not is beside the point. The reality is that for five years I have not been with any man who even came close to connecting with me as Yaro does. To me, that's more confirmation than the philosophy of destiny."

"I have to agree with you there, Mom. In fact, I have wondered about you not being involved with anyone for so long. You must admit, it's not your MO." Claire certainly wasn't hostile or incredulous, thus Leisa was relieved that she was right to predict that her daughter would give this development in her mother's life a shot. "But what about these past five years? What has he been doing? Where? Actually no, back up and tell me who he is. Is this going to be something like the movie, *Guess Who Is Coming To Dinner*, with that handsome Sidney Poiter?"

They both laughed and Leisa nodded affirmatively. "Just as handsome, but much darker. He is a tall, slim, muscular man with the blackest eyes one can imagine. He was a Fulbright Scholarship winner and speaks several languages. He was getting his masters degree in Educational

110

Leadership as I was, and he returned to his country, Burkina Faso, to help advance his country's educational system. I have no idea what he has done since he returned; only what his intention was." Now, for the hard part, thought Leisa, as she took another sip of wine and cleared her throat. "I need to be completely honest and tell you the 'rest of the story' as that famous radio news commentator says. When we met he was married, and he is twelve years younger than me."

"Oh Mom, no! This story isn't like the movie then at all."

Quickly Leisa responded, "Well we don't know that for sure. Yes, he will always be younger than me and a black man, and I realize that those two things are no-no's in our culture. However, something must have changed about his being married. When we parted, it was agreed that we would not communicate unless it was appropriate, and we didn't. The fact that he has contacted me now means that something has changed. He would not explain over the phone, but he will when we see each other in July."

Claire was silent for a minute, but slowly she started smiling. "Oh, Mom. You have always lived outside the box, but this is really something. I can only imagine the bad press you are going to get around here. Unsophisticated ranchers and their forever wives, friends with small uneventful lives, and a son who can't deal with you even dating."

"Oh, I know, for sure (Yaro says that all the time). Three verbotens all in one package: a married man, a younger man, and a black man."

"Well, for sure, (like you say Yaro says all the time), you can count on me being in your corner. As a matter of fact, I wouldn't miss this trauma/drama for anything. You realize that we don't get much excitement out here in the country. And, as you know, I prefer it that way." Claire laughed as she got up to refill their wine glasses. She returned with a question, "Are you planning on telling my big brother this weekend?"

"Not hardly. I think it would be best if I wait until I know the whole story. So, when I get back from New York, I'll tell him then. I'll take photos of our week there, and I will have a plan to share with you guys. I don't know, but at the same time I do know, that this is not just a visit because he is in the country. We are going to put our lives together and it is not one minute too soon. I have never been so thrilled or so sure about anything in my life."

Mother and daughter just sat in silence sipping their wine for a few minutes. The sun was down now and the evening shadows came through the windows. If Leisa was ever going to be depressed, this was the time of day for it. But not this day! Her faith in Claire's willingness to hear whatever needed to be revealed, and her 'allowing' spirit had been confirmed. Leisa had never been prouder of her only daughter, or more relieved by her attitude.

"Mom, I trust that you know what you are doing. All these five years, and you haven't been attracted to anyone else, plus it sounds like there really is some kind of unique connection between the two of you. Besides, you certainly won't be moving in next door, so to speak, so if you can get past your son, no one else really matters, do they?"

"Absolutely not! However, you know that I would want my friends and family to approve of me, and it will bother me if they don't. I know it shouldn't, (at least that is what all the books say), but I know myself well enough to know that I am a pleaser. Nevertheless, there is no contest here. I would never let 'what people think' keep me from Yaro. We are going to be together. How, where, and when is a mystery to me today, but it won't be for much longer. I am just so glad that I decided to retire this past May. That makes me free to pack."

Claire reached over and gave her mom a hug and said, "My mother, the outside-the-box lady." She turned to listen and then continued, "Come on, I think I hear the sunshine girls. Let's go see if they caught any fish. And try to do something about the way your face is glowing."

* * * * *

Once again Leisa found herself making arrangements for a romantic rendezvous, only this time it was to celebrate a beginning, not create a memory for an ending. Five years ago in Arizona her heavy heart had kept her from appreciating the farewell dinner in Sedona, where they spent their last private time together. But not now! She was beside herself with joy as she perused the hotel listings on the web, and made her flight reservations. Thank goodness Kitty was in California visiting her children because she didn't want to tell anyone else about Yaro – not until she knew what their future was. Keeping all her planning and shopping a secret from Kitty would have been impossible. If only she could sleep, life would be perfect.

After much shopping on the web, she decided that 'On The Ave' Hotel on the Upper West Side would be perfect. She loved the unusual name. Over and over again she read the description of the hotel: "The contemporary styling of On The Ave Hotel is manifested by a lobby with polished wood floor, plush-fabric seating, and a banquette alcove with tufted upholstered wall. Easy-listening music plays in the background. Furnished with greenery, flowers (in summer), dining sets, and sunbathing lounge chairs, a balcony on the top floor supplies sweeping views of the city and Central Park. On Sundays, Green Flea Market sets up outdoors at West 77th Street and Columbus Avenue, two blocks away."

Leisa liked the description of the rooms too. Not fancy, but luxurious. Their website advertised, "....there are 267 guestrooms with large windows in a 16-story building. Guests may enjoy a balcony overlooking the city on the top floor. Belgian chocolates with turndown service, and complimentary Godiva coffee," this sounded especially good to her because a cup of coffee was always the first order of business for any day.

Leisa also spent some time researching Central Park. She had never been there, but that would be no excuse. She had learned the hard way that Yaro will have a million questions about everything. When they had gone to the Grand Canyon and Lake Powell together, she had embarrassed herself by being so ignorant of the history of both. That wouldn't happen again. Thanks to the web, anyone could learn about anything in a hurry. And, what she didn't know about Central Park would fill a book. Thank goodness she loved history so it wasn't a chore to read about the park, thus she read....

114

Central Park was the first landscaped public park in the United States. Advocates of creating the park – primarily wealthy merchants and landowners – admired the public grounds of London and Paris and urged that New York needed a comparable facility to establish its international reputation. A public park, they argued, would offer their own families an attractive setting for carriage rides and provide working-class New Yorkers with a healthy alternative to the saloon. After three years of debate over the park site and cost, in 1853 the state legislature authorized the City of New York to use the power of eminent domain to acquire more than 700 acres of land in the center of Manhattan.

An irregular terrain of swamps and bluffs, punctuated by rocky outcroppings, made the land between Fifth and Eighth avenues and 59th and 106th streets undesirable for private development. Creating the park, however, required displacing roughly 1,600 poor residents, including Irish pig farmers and German gardeners, who lived in shanties on the site. At Eighth Avenue and 82nd Street, Seneca Village had been one of the city's most stable African-American settlements, with three churches and a school. The extension of the boundaries to 110th Street in 1863 brought the park to its current 843 acres.

Leisa considered the fact that they would be in New York City for a week, so certainly they will get to see the main tourist attractions. She was glad that she had never been there, because now they will experience it together.

'Together' was THE word these days, she realized as she looked up from the book to watch it rain outside. She wanted to do everything with Yaro. His call had awaken a hunger in her that was ravenous. They would most certainly be out in the city seeing marvelous things, but their being together would make the day, regardless of what they were touring. So as she read about the American Museum of Natural History, the Metropolitan Museum of Art, Rockefeller Center, Times Square, and Harlem – all nearby points of interest, she fantasized about them being together. Since he had said to choose a hotel near the park, no doubt, he will want to visit the famous zoo, and she will want to see Shakespeare in the Park at the Delacorte Theater, the most celebrated open air theater in the park. So on this rainy afternoon in Houston, in her favorite bookstore, Barnes and Nobles on 610 Loop, she enjoyed a book devoted to New York City's places. As she looked at the many pictures of Central Park, she could just see the two of them strolling by the beautiful centerpiece of the park, Bethesda Terrace, to the more rustic charm of the North Woods. They could have another picnic together. This time, instead of Bell Rock in Arizona, they will sit on the lawn and watch the beautiful swans on the lake. Life was truly a banquet, mused Leisa, as she closed the book about New York she had enjoyed all afternoon. Yes, five years ago it was the majestic mountains and canyons of Arizona to the sunsets over Lake Powell, now next week it would be the streets of Manhattan. And the thrill of it all derived from the pleasure of his company. She smiled as she stretched herself out of the comfortable chair and headed out the door to Shotsy who had been

116

waiting in the wet parking lot. As she unlocked the door and sat down behind the steering wheel, she realized that this man was not just icing. She smiled to herself and announced to Shotsy, "I am ready to confess to you and the entire world that Yaro Bomou is and will always be the major ingredient in my cake."

CHAPTER NINE

The hotel room was perfect, Leisa decided, as she inspected it carefully. She especially liked the balcony. It was early afternoon, so she was just looking out at a huge city, and realizing that tonight they would be served their first meal together in five years here under the stars. As she unpacked her clothes and makeup, she decided to try to rest for at least an hour before taking a bubble bath and getting dressed. Yaro's plane wasn't due in for another three hours, so she had plenty of time to get ready and then go down to the hotel lobby for a glass of wine while she waited. She knew she wouldn't sleep, but she was going to try anyway.

She couldn't believe it! "Good lord, I've been asleep", she said to herself, as she stared at the clock beside the bed. "That can't be right," she insisted, as she looked at the time on her cell phone. But it was. Leisa had been asleep for over an hour. "Oh, thank you God," she said as she got out of bed. "Sleep was the only thing I needed. I look ten years younger after every nap," she laughed as she inspected herself in the bathroom mirror.

She found the music channels on the TV and chose the romantic classics to listen to as she enjoyed her bubble bath. She knew her heart was pounding, but it wasn't until she was applying eyeliner that she noticed that her hands were shaking too. She tried to remember a time when she was more aroused by the prospect of an evening, and she couldn't. She tried to visualize what he would look like now, and she could. He would have the same body, and maybe his face might show some evidence of years, but at thirty five she couldn't imagine that he would be much changed.

"And, what about you," she asked the mirror. "What will Yaro see when he looks at you? I wonder how forty seven will look to him?"

Leisa had always taken her good looks for granted. She had been a beauty all her life, so she was somewhat slightly surprised when anyone commented on how she never aged. Her weight never changed; she had inherited her mother's flawless skin, and most importantly, her spirit got younger every year instead of older. However, she had two secret weapons against aging that she would share when asked, and she had been asked more than once. Every time she did though, the woman or women would dismiss them as unrealistic. Nevertheless, she gave the same answer every time: Transcendental Meditation, practiced twice a day, retards the aging process. Research proves that the twenty minutes of meditation, twice a day, is equivalent to eight hours of sound sleep. Everyone knows that when you are asleep your body repairs itself, so it is a no-brainer.

The other weapon against aging can't be proven like the effects of meditation can. No, it was a mind thing. Leisa had learned years ago that what we think becomes our reality. Our habitual way of thinking actually manifests in our physical body. Therefore, if one can refuse to buy into all the hype about aging; doesn't make a habit of lamenting it in conversation, and thinks of themselves as adults, not senior citizens – they won't be. Needless to say, she had never gotten any takers, but that hadn't stopped her from proclaiming it whenever the subject came up. And, her body continued to testify to the truth of it. Of course, no one believed her. They were positive that her perpetual youth-fulness was courtesy of her mother's DNA. And of course, it helped, admitted Leisa, as she pulled on her size six designer jeans from Yoakum, Texas' Double-D Ranch Wear. She was just doing her part by helping her genes along with her way of thinking about age. Never before had it mattered. She put on her high-heeled sandals after buttoning the soft, feminine, blouse of aqua silk and surveyed her image in the full-length mirror in the spacious bathroom. No one would believe she was forty seven. However, the arithmetic couldn't be changed, and in a culture where the man was supposed to be older than the woman, what one looked like or felt like was of little consequence. It still mattered.

"Leisa, live in the moment," she told herself as she checked to see if she had the room key in her handbag. "You look like a million dollars tonight, and that is what counts. And with any luck, Babe, you will have years to prove everyone wrong."

The pianist in the lobby was drawing a crowd when Leisa sat down with her glass of wine. Dimmed lights, romantic music, admiring glances and the prospect of Yaro's call any minute now had her on top of the world. Regardless of what lies ahead for me, she thought as she smiled at the pianist, life will never be any more abundant than it is at this moment. There was no doubt that she and Yaro would pick up right where they left off, so she had zero concern about how it would be between them. The heart pounding and the hands shaking had only to do with the thrill of finally getting to see him again.

The phone rang and she heard him say, "I am in your country. Diarabi, we are almost together again. Give me the name of the hotel so I can tell the cab driver. Where will you be?"

"Tell the driver it is the On The Ave Hotel. Come to our room, number 1608." Leisa's voice was husky with desire.

"Good! I am coming. For sure, I am coming." His voice was almost a whisper. A slight silence followed and then he said in a stronger, less personal voice, "I will hang up now and watch the city." Click went the phone. Funny how she had forgotten that Yaro never said goodbye over the phone. Yes, he could be a man of few words, she thought, as she took another sip of wine and turned her attention to the music. Life doesn't get any better than this.

Leisa opened the door. He looked the same. For a split second his tall, erect, slim body remained motionless, but his eyes were wide with wonder and filled with anticipation. The sound of releasing years of longing escaped his lips as he enveloped her in his arms. His strong body held her up and off the floor as he twirled them into the room. The kiss she had waited years for was happening, and there were no thoughts. Leisa was not thinking! There was only the moment, and it was not cluttered with anything but passion.

Words were slow in coming. After their initial embrace and kiss inside the door, Leisa led the way into the room and motioned for him to join her on the love-seat. He didn't take his eyes off her. Clearly, he wasn't aware of anything else in the room but her. Lovingly and gently, Yaro again took her in his arms and seconds later his first words were, "Diarabi, you are almost as beautiful as you are loved."

Leisa looked up at him as she acknowledged the compliment with a smile, but she intuitively knew that it was not time to talk about their reunion. They were together and that was enough. She was satisfied to just sit in his embrace and feel him.

He lowered his head to put his mouth on her breast as he cupped it in his hand. She wasn't wearing a bra and the blouse material was very soft, so the sensation permeated through the fabric. Seconds passed in silence before she realized he was crying. She felt his sobs as they got stronger and his arms were getting tighter and tighter around her. Without a word, he got up and went into the bathroom, and when he returned he chose to sit on the bed away from her. His explanation came out as he stared at her unblinkingly.

"My tears are a paradox. They are for the joy I feel to finally be with you after all these years, yet they are also for how my marriage to Anzounou ended."

Leisa watched him get up and walk to the sliding glass door to the balcony. He looked out for a minute, but didn't open it. Instead, he turned back to Leisa and began his story.

"I never stopped to consider the possibility that my

wife was unfulfilled too. I was so wrapped up in my longing for you that it never occurred to me that she deserved the same passion for someone that I had for you. I filled my years with furthering my education and career accomplishments, and cared for her as my friend, the mother of my child and partner in the life we had planned since our marriage. She had to be the one to ultimately risk speaking the truth that I could then admit to, and that fact has left me feeling impotent. Yes, am I nothing but a weak, powerless, hapless man? Would I have spent the rest of my days begging Allah to intervene, if she hadn't taken the action necessary to remedy our lives?"

Leisa knew not to move. Instead, of going to him and offering comfort, she felt that she should just stay on the couch where she was. He stood there staring at her for what seemed like a long time. Then he walked over to the bed and slumped down on it, heavy with exhaustion. She immediately joined him, and they laid down there side by side in the dusk of the day, without any words being spoken.

Finally, she decided to share what she was thinking. "It has been my experience that men tend to refrain from speaking what's in their hearts. I don't personally think it is because they are cowardly. No, it is because society has conditioned them to think of themselves as in control, thus their responsibilities to others come before all else. Not even an undying passion for someone or some radically different life opportunity prompts them to instigate change. So, instead of faulting yourself for failing to own up to your secret lost love, be grateful that Anzounou was willing to risk leaving the comfort of the known for what she wanted for herself. A marriage without passion was not good enough for her, and she had what it took to tell you so. That is the reality of it. To spend any more time wishing it had been otherwise is pointless. Nothing in the past can be changed except your perception of it. The years you had together provided you both with what you now have to go forward with your lives. If you need to believe that all is according to Allah's plan, why not give Him credit for how it went? My suggestion to you now, Yaro, would be to not let your masculine ego deprive you of another minute's thankfulness for what is."

He did not speak, but immediately there was movement towards her that brought them closer. She was laying on her back so he put an arm and his leg across her body and his face into the nape of her neck. Minutes passed in silence before his breathing changed, and Leisa realized he was asleep. She had a good view of the sky in its beginnings of dusk, so she enjoyed watching it change as she lay very still so he could rest.

Her earlier nap and the high energy around their togetherness had her wide awake. Questions – so many questions: Why was Yaro in New York City? Who was paying 500 dollars a day for a week's stay in this hotel? His divorce couldn't just automatically put them together for the rest of their lives. She wouldn't fit in his world any more than he would fit in her southern one. And what about his daughter, or more children, for all she knew? There was much, much more to this story, she thought, as she listened to him breathe and felt the weight of his arm and leg over her. And, par usual, Leisa eventually went to planning ahead for when he would wake up. Thank goodness she had ordered a small tray of cheeses, fruit and a variety of bread slices, with both wine and sparkling water. It was much too early for dinner, but he might be hungry for a light snack. And for her too, she hoped. Maybe now that he had told her what had happened to his marriage, he would feel free to make love to her.

He opened his eyes and moved over to sit up. He had slept over an hour. After a long stretch and a soft sigh, he turned to look at her and said, "Ah, Diarabi, you are here. This is not a dream." His voice was like satin and his eyes were luminous. "Are you ready for a shower?"

There were two water heads, opposite each other. The blue and silver marble provided the touch of class to the large shower with its curved seat in one corner. She had never felt more desirable, even with her soaked hair and the carefully applied makeup going down the drain. Yaro had a way of looking at her that exuded sexuality. He was the only man she had ever known who could so effectively make love with his eyes.

"Your body is beautiful, as I knew it would be," he said softly. He ran his hands down over her breasts and slowly past her stomach to linger on her upper thighs. Then as he sat down on the marble bench, his arms went around behind her lower back to firmly pull her wet body to his face. She raised one of her legs so she could place it around him, thus helping his large, strong mouth take her. The water was pouring over them as their desire for each other made them one. They were finally together in every sense of the word. Needless to say, being a white woman from the South, she had never seen a black man's naked body. His was without an ounce of fat; only firm muscles. His blackness totally captivated her. He sensed that she was now totally engulfed with experiencing him as her lover. It was clear to him that she was intoxicated with joy, totally greedy for everything. Maybe there is such a thing as destiny, was Leisa's last thought before she completely left her head and became only her body.

She was too excited to eat, but Yaro was glad to have the tray of snacks. They were both in the Frette Italian terrycloth bathrobes provided by the hotel, sitting on the balcony waiting for the meal they had ordered. Thank goodness the evening light was complimentary to Leisa's face, because putting on new makeup after the shower seemed like a waste of precious time. The lights of the city drew them to the balcony wall. She was sipping her wine and he was standing behind her with his arms around her waist. "Ah Diarabi, what a beautiful place this is. For sure, our new home, how very beautiful."

"Our new home? New York City? Really.....well, that's fine.....that will work, but isn't it time for a few details like when and why this city?"

He led her over to the two lounge chairs before explaining. "Ah, Diarabi, you are looking at a man who has been hired to work at the United Nations in the International Bureau of Education, which is affiliated with UNESCO. I take my position there in a week." His melancholy eyes were gone, Leisa noted. No longer was he living in the past. No self incrimination or regrets, instead he was alive and transported. In fact, she was so relieved to see the change in

126

him, that what he was saying almost didn't register with her.

"You what? Did you say that you have a job with the UN?" she sounded confused and that was because she was confused.

"For sure, yes! I begin my work next week at UN Headquarters. I was contacted over three months past to consider a post in UNESCO. I am in your country Diarabi, to stay. I am to be here at last."

Leisa was incredulous and her joy propelled her off the lounge and into his lap. "How perfect! How absolutely perfect. What will you be doing at the UN? I'm sure it must have to do with education."

He was holding her tight and started to untie her robe when she laughingly stopped him. "No you don't. I have got to know a few more details before you take over my body again, and besides our dinner will be here soon. So talk! Tell me about the job," she laughingly demanded, as she attempted to free herself of him.

"Ah! Orders, I am given orders only hours after I arrive. Don't you understand that I am the boss?" The mirth in his eyes gave him away.

Leisa joined in the fun with her Texas version of "Oh....for sure". She got off his lap and retied her bathrobe, then moved back to her lounge and picked up the glass of wine. "Shoot, as they say in Texas. Tell me your job description."

Yaro smiled at her and sighed. "This is my dream. I am living my dream." He sat for just a second and gazed at her lovingly. Then he began his explanation. "My job has to do with curriculum development for the developing countries of the world. There are five different aspects of this, and at this time it has not been determined which one I'll be heading. Therefore, let me tell you about all five". Leisa smiled to herself and sipped her wine as she watched him go from lover to professional educator right in front of her eyes.

"One possibility is that I'll be involved with organizing training activities and providing technical advice to strengthen capacities in critical areas of curriculum design, planning and renewal. Or, I might be facilitating regional networking and exchange among experts from national curriculum departments. Another possibility is the job of promoting action-research activities addressing curriculum development in post-conflict and transition countries. Or, they could have me developing modules, training tools and resource materials in curriculum policy-making and development. Or lastly, I could be working towards the constitution of a *Global Curriculum Network* representing a world wide community of practitioners devoted to curriculum development. I'll know next week when I report to work," he ended.

The door bell buzzed, and dinner was served. Small talk was now needed if she was going to be able to swallow her food, so Leisa deliberately avoided all the many questions still left unanswered and chose a subject that would not be highly charged emotionally. "I have had some time to research the city's tourist attractions and I'm hoping that we can begin tomorrow to enjoy them. How about the park? Central Park? Would you want to spend the day there together?" When did she become so hungry she wondered, as she took another bite of filet mignon?

"For sure, let us enjoy the whole day there." Yaro too was hungry and visibly relaxed. No need to rush with all the untold stories. They had a lifetime now to share them. Leisa would hold in check her habit of rushing with everything. The stars were out; the lamp light from their room was just enough light for dining; the love of her life was back, and she was rejoicing in her soul.

Yaro was tired from his long plane flight and the rest from his earlier nap was spent. Therefore, not long after they had finished dinner he was ready to go to bed. Leisa was too excited to sleep, but she was totally happy to lay there and listen to his measured breathing. Eventually, she too joined him in sleep. As the night's hours passed, he would be asleep, and then he would be awake and making love to her. His body would awaken hers, again and again for possession. Seldom were any words spoken. Their bodies were starved for each other, and their minds didn't seem to be involved. Leisa had never been as satisfied by a lover. When the sunlight came through the patio glass door and signaled the morning, she had never been so ready for her cup of coffee.

Leisa did her TM while he performed his morning prayer ritual, then they were ready for breakfast in their room. Yaro was rested and his lighthearted, sunny disposition was contagious. In the light of this beautiful new day she decided it was time to continue with the mystery, so Leisa broached the subject of his plans for them by asking, "Last night you said that New York City would be our home. Let's talk about that."

"Oh, Diarabi, I won't make that decision for the both of us. It is just that I don't know where else people live who

129

work here in Manhattan. Do you know? What would you suggest?"

"Well it depends on if you are talking about only you and me. If so, then a city apartment would be fine, but if there are children, then a family home out of the city would be better. You haven't mentioned anything about your children." Leisa said hesitantly. She hated to see his good humor ruined by a painful subject, but she didn't see any way around it.

Yaro's eyes welled with tears. "Ah, my Ana. I have only the one child and she will be living with Anzounou. Her mother and I are completely agreeable concerning our daughter. Ana will live with Anzounou, but every three months there is a one month recess from school. During that time, three times a year, she will come to stay with us. This plan felt familiar to Ana because she is conditioned to being without me. You see, not only was I in Arizona for two years when she was a baby, but I was in France for three years getting my PhD from the time she was five to eight. Actually, I don't believe that Ana has any negative under-standing of our divorce because there is no strife or unhappiness expressed between her mother and me. Too, having a home in both the United States and France will only add to her education and life experiences."

"Well then, if we are going to be a family we must look at real estate outside the city." Leisa's mind took off like a bullet. "As it happens, I have a friend who lives in Westfield, New Jersey and she has always been happy there. What do you think? I'm really not very informed about the smaller towns that encircle New York, but we can always find out."

"For sure, we can investigate for the best place. After this week, I have a one bedroom suite at the Beekman Tower Hotel for two months. After that time, the UN will not be responsible for my housing. Can you stay with me? Must you return to Texas next week? Wait a minute and I'll get the brochure I was given on the hotel so you can read about it."

"Don't be silly," laughed Leisa, as he went to his briefcase. "Of course I'll have to return to Texas. I only brought two pairs of jeans." Was she actually planning to leave her family and move across the country to begin yet another life? He handed her the brochure and went back to finishing his breakfast. What a beautiful hotel, thought Leisa, as she looked at the photos and read....*a New York landmark...built in 1928.....an art deco icon located a few short steps from the UN.....spacious suites reflect traditional styling.....terraces and inspiring river views.* Yaro pointed out that they would have the one bedroom suite with a luxurious living room, dining area and a separate bedroom. A small kitchen would be sufficient, and there were two restaurants in the hotel.

"Seriously though, I can settle my affairs in Houston in short order because what I really need to do is get cracking on finding a teaching job. School will be starting here the end of next month." Nothing made her happier than a whole new life to plan. With Yaro starting a new job next week, they would have to spend this one making major life decisions, TOGETHER. It was fast becoming Leisa's favorite word.

By lunch time they had spent a couple of tourist type hours in Central Park. Eating a hotdog there was a required experience, so as they sat on the grass to eat, Leisa easily and naturally stepped into her planning director role. "Yaro, I have relocated numerous times and I can tell you that the first thing to do is determine where you are going to live. Then, one looks for work. Since you have your job, I'll be the one hoofing it. My monthly retirement money won't be near enough for us to live comfortably in this part of the country. Now, if it was Texas that would be different, but not here. Mercy no! I've got to get a teaching job."

"How can you teach now? You told me on the phone when I called you from Burkina Faso that you were retiring early so you could get started on your PhD. It won't do at all for you to abort that plan."

It warmed her heart to realize that he had remembered. "Not to worry about that. I can always begin it in a year or two. First we must know what it will cost us to live here. I have always lived in the western states, so I have no clue, but I do have a suspicion that it is going to be expensive. What are the facts? Like, are you going to tell me your salary or is that a state secret," teased Leisa.

"Oh, for sure. It is a fortune in my country, but you will have to tell me if I can afford a wife here." He too could joke. Actually, it was the first time he had made any reference to marriage. Not that there was any question about it, but it did get Leisa's attention. "My salary is to be one hundred fifty thousand a year with full benefits for myself and my family," he announced with a mixture of pride and uncertainty. "Is that a good amount for life here in your

United States?"

"With a teacher's salary, plus my retirement, and your salary I do believe we will be in clover," she replied gaily. "Our biggest expense is going to be housing. Maybe we better contact a realtor and find out what the real estate prices are here.....where ever 'here' is going to be."

Yaro was faking a frown, "One of these days when we have time, you must take the time to explain your language to me. 'Shoot', like in Texas. What is that? Then you say we are in clover. What is 'clover'? And, what is 'hoofing it' and get 'cracking'? He wiped his mouth and reached over to give her a light kiss on the cheek. Then he acted shocked at himself, "Look what you do to me? I am kissing you in public. Oh for sure, I am a new man."

Leisa laughed as she quickly kissed him back. "You are going to make a fine American, and not to worry, I will have you speaking the lingo in no time."

There wasn't time to research all the possible towns around New York City, she had argued, so without considering any other town, they found themselves the next day on the commuter train to Westfield, New Jersey to meet a realtor. As they traveled, Leisa read the information they had gotten off the internet about the small town, while Yaro watched the passing American scene. She would read selected information to him as he stared out the window. "It says here that Westfield is approximately 25 miles southwest of New York City, and its population is forty thousand. It's old too, Yaro. The area was settled in the late 17th century as part of the Elizabethtown Tract, but that's enough history for today. We need to know the current stuff. Let's see.....downtown features many local shops and chain stores. It says here....are you listening?............ that Downtown Westfield, with over 200 retail establishments and 400 commercial enterprises, is a regional destination in New Jersey. In 2004, Westfield won the Great American Main Street Award from the National Trust. Look at this picture, Yaro. I love the way the small town atmosphere has been preserved with trees and benches on the main street."

Yaro took the paper she was extending to him and smiled at her. "You are so beautiful. Your country too is beautiful and my life is beautiful. Praise be to Allah." Then he took his gaze off Leisa and looked at the picture of Main Street and added, "This town too is beautiful."

It was his first mention of Allah since the night he arrived. Leisa found it unrealistic to make religion such a constant in one's life, but she left the subject alone. They would have decades to delve into the relationship between man and the Divine – by whatever name.

Instead she said, "Now listen up because this is most important. New Jersey Transit's Raritan Valley Line provides rail service from the Westfield train station to Newark Penn Station in Newark with connecting service to Penn Station New York. Westfield's position and schedule on the Raritan Valley line make it highly desirable for commuters, as several times in the morning and evening rush hours a non-stop service is operated to and from the Newark transfer station. On these non-stop services, the one-way journey time to and from New York Penn Station is 50 minutes."

"Does this mean that I can go from our home in

Westfield to my office in New York City without getting into a car?"

"Only if you want to walk or ride a bicycle from the house to the train station, and I don't think that will happen. It gets very cold here with snow and ice. But, not to worry, my dear, I'll drive you until you have a license and we have another car." She gave him another quick, friendly kiss right there in front of God and everyone else in the train car. Maybe with time she would regain her sophisticated, I-know-how-to-behave-in-public ways, but for now she couldn't. With the nights made for love-making and the days for life-making, her reality was perfect.

By the second trip to Westfield they had located their house. It was an easy choice, and they both recognized it as the right one as soon as they saw it. The neighborhood was an older one so the oak trees were giant and the houses had been built in the 1950's. It was a small two-story white house with a red roof, front door and shutters. And, of all things, it had a white picketed fence around the back yard. The large fireplace was right in the center of the living room, and the two bedrooms were upstairs. The other houses they looked at were much newer and larger. So much so, that Yaro was not even comfortable in them. Now Leisa, on the other hand, liked space. Being from Texas, she had always 'done' space. However, when she realized the difference in cost, space was painlessly sacrificed for the smaller price tag. So the realtor was left with the promise that they would make an offer on the house as soon as Leisa had signed a teaching contract. With her good credit, both salaries and no debt, they would easily qualify.

"Tell me about your home in Ouagadougou," Leisa asked as they were taking the commuter train back into Manhattan. "Did you sell it?"

"Yes. One of the professors I taught with at the university purchased it at a good price. Anzounou and I marveled at how every thing just seemed to fall into place, once the dye was cast."

Just two days before she had to fly back to Texas, Leisa got an audience with the director of the Westfield Public Schools Human Resources Department. Yaro was waiting for her on the front steps of the historical old building. He could tell as he watched her come towards him that things had gone well.

"I knew there would be a position for me, and it is teaching world history to sophomores – my favorite subject and grade level. I felt it in my bones before I ever sat down," Leisa was having a hard time maintaining her decorum. "This is what I call Divine Order, Yaro. No one on this planet is in control, like we insist on thinking we are. Life goes the way it goes, and it has been my experience that it is for our highest good. My challenge with this arrangement is that when something is happening that is so painful and unwanted, I am tempted to rail against God or beg Him to fix whatever it is that I think is wrong. In the past, I have often felt victimized instead of trusting and being allowing of what is." Immediately, she hesitated and Yaro stopped walking too. "I'm sorry," she finished lamely. "All my friends and family will tell you I have this habit of explaining how life works when any fool knows it is all a mystery. I'm sorry," she said again.

"Diarabi, learn today that you can always speak your truth to me. If I do not agree or understand, that will only create conversation, not a problem between us." They were standing on the sidewalk under a shady tree only a few steps away from Westfield's Public School District building. He took her hand and pressed it to his lips. "We will always have so much to talk about, and for sure, that is a good thing."

It was their last train trip back into Manhattan, and both of them seemed a little consumed by the day's events. After Leisa's meeting at the administration office, they had enjoyed a light lunch at a sidewalk café in downtown Westfield before catching the train back to New York. Now, as the familiar scenes passed by, silence reigned. Leisa was busy making a mental list of all the paper work she would need to gather and mail to Human Resources, because she couldn't actually sign a teaching contract until she did. They had agreed to not make an offer on the house and put down earnest money until the teaching contract was signed. She was thinking about what to do with all her brand new furniture, (would it be a good idea to ask her son to haul it cross country in his huge covered cattle trailer to save the cost of a moving van?), when Yaro interrupted her with a new subject.

"Diarabi, tell me about transpersonal psychology. I know nothing about it, but I suspect that it has much to do with the way you think".

Leisa smiled at him and his way of giving a subject private consideration before asking about it. She knew that this request for information had directly to do with what she had said outside the administration building that morning. Once again here was confirmation that he was the right man for her because one of her main disappointments with other men had been that they were never interested in how she thought. Or, they were threatened by it and thus wouldn't discuss it. "For sure," she teased in her exaggerated Texas drawl, "I can certainly do that." Would she ever get over wanting to kiss him constantly, she wondered as she looked at his mouth.

She began. "I was sitting in a doctor's office last fall reading a Psychology Today magazine when I came across an advertisement for Westbrook University, a distance learning accredited institution. Transpersonal psychology was among the several PhD degrees offered, and it was a surprise to me that such a degree existed, yet immediately clear that this is what I wanted to study. I have always been a student of human behavior, but never satisfied with the traditional college psychology courses I had taken. So, I went on the internet to do research and was convinced that this is what I would do next. Unlike you, I don't have a clue how I will use it, but get it I must."

"And that is why I question you deciding to put it off," Yaro interrupted. "Are you sure you want to make that sacrifice?"

"Dear, it is not a sacrifice. We need more than re-tirement income from me now, so the perfect job was waiting for me. When the time is right, I will know it and thus begin my studies. Now, let me tell you what it is." She noticed that she was beginning to use 'dear' as her term of endearment.

"Transpersonal psychology studies the transcendent or spiritual aspect of the human experience. It is the study of humanity's highest potential, and with the recognition, understanding, and realization of unitive, spiritual, and transcendent states of consciousness. Yaro, I have reviewed the several definitions that have appeared in literature over the period of 1969 to 1991 and found that five key themes in particular featured prominently in these definitions: states of consciousness, higher or ultimate potential, beyond the ego or personal self, transcendence and the spiritual. Maybe you have heard of some of the thinkers who have contributed to this relatively new branch of psychology: William James, Sigmund Freud, Carl Jung, and Abraham Maslow?"

"I have studied Maslow because some of his work is incorporated into approaches in education, and I know of Freud and Jung, but not James," Yaro replied.

"Well, it isn't necessary to know their work." Leisa continued. "What I do want you to understand is that transpersonal psychology is sometimes confused with the New Age Movement. Although it has many overlapping interests with theories and thinkers associated with the term "new age", it is still problematic to place transpersonal psychology within such a framework. It is an academic discipline, not a religious or spiritual movement. Too, Yaro, you need to know that transpersonal psychology has its critics. Some psychologists are concerned about the low level of reflection on the dark side of human nature, and on human suffering. And the other thing is, that religious and spiritual experiences have in the past been seen as either regressive or pathological and treated as such. Anyway, the

139

bottom line for me is that I resonate with the subject in all its forms and will pursue the study of it one day." The train was pulling into Penn Station and once again it was time to retire the day.

"Are you asleep?" asked Leisa quietly.

"Nooooooo, not really."

"Good. I just wanted to hear more about Ana, but only if you feel like talking about her now."

Yaro's voice was immediately stronger and energized. "Ah, my angel, Ana. For sure, you will be great friends. At first it will be because you will be such an oddity to her, and she will be intent on figuring you out. At a very young age we noticed that she most enjoyed seeking out what she didn't know or understand. She asks a million questions...I know, like me.... and her talent for languages was noted early on. However, her high intelligence does not interfere with her being a mischievous child sometimes. Despite her brilliance, she has gotten a fair share of spankings. Physically she is very tall for her age; slim, and she is most proud of her heavy head of black hair. Unlike me, her skin is not so black."

"Won't they all be so darling together?" interjected Leisa. "My two granddaughters are tall and very blond; in fact, we refer to them collectively as the sunshine girls. They are all about the same age, so can't you just see the three of them running us ragged when Ana is here? And don't you think for one minute that I will be the only oddity around our house. My granddaughters won't know what to make of you," she teased as she grabbed his hand and put it on her breast. More love. She wanted more love. "Am I wearing you out?" she asked as he willingly moved toward her.

* * * * *

It was to be their last night together before she returned to Texas, thus a very special occasion. Yaro suggested that they go to dinner at the Top of the Tower Restaurant. He wanted Leisa to see the hotel where they would be living during the time it would take to get into their house in Westfield. No jeans tonight. The brochure advertised fine American cuisine in an elegant setting, with live piano music, and a spectacular view of the New York City skyline. Thank goodness she had brought one cocktail dress hoping for such an occasion. She had Yaro wait out on the balcony while she got dressed. The perfect black dress, with its plunging neckline and long straight skirt was dramatic. He had never seen her so dressed up before and it thrilled her to death to see the notice he took of her. The door bell interrupted their compliments of each other, (he had on one of the three new suits they had selected earlier in the week), and Yaro moved to answer it. He had ordered flowers for her, and with a smile devoid of all the uncertainty of the first time he presented her with flowers, he gave them to her.

"Oh how beautiful," Leisa whispered as she took the red roses in her hands. "You are just the most thoughtful, romantic man."

"Would you say they are an improvement over the first ones?" It was more of a statement than a question to be answered.

"No and yes." Leisa replied quickly. "I still have those plastic flowers you gave me years ago, and I will never part with them. They were perfect then; these are perfect now."

The dining scene was right out of a romance novel, thought Leisa, as she returned from the powder room. Candlelight shone on snow white linen cloths graced with fresh flowers. The tables were arranged in a semi-circle around the small dance floor. The grand piano was on an elevated podium with bar stools provided for up-close-and-personal listeners.

Yaro had ordered wine for her and as she walked to their table she could see that he was enjoying some sparkling water. His gaze on her was completely revealing. No one in that room had any doubt that they were TOGETHER. The black and the white of it, she thought, as their eyes connected. Who was that woman in Arizona with all the trauma/drama around the color of his skin? When had her prejudice vanished, and why? The answer was obvious. It was her thoughts, her way of thinking that had changed, certainly not Yaro. He was still a black man, yet as she walked in front of all the people in the dining room towards their table, she felt such pride to be with him. Evidence that it is our thoughts that create our reality, not external conditions. Such a simple truth, yet one that eludes many people. On Bell Rock in Sedona years ago, Leisa was loath to think that the other people who were on the mountain with them that day would take them to be a couple. Now she was ready to announce to the world, (and specifically her Texas family), their love for each other and plan to spend the rest of their lives together.

The music was so inviting and she wanted to dance. God knows, she was born dancing, but she had no idea how Yaro felt about it. Then as if he had read her mind, he said, "It is time we danced together." With the finesse of a maestro, he led her to the dance floor and took her into his arms like she was a precious piece of china. Their bodies touched and he hesitated just a split second while he murmured, "Diarabi, I love you." Then he moved her with his body to the tune of "Some Romantic Evening".

Like the late-night movies, it was the classic, enchanted, dinner date. Beautiful people, delicious food, the New York skyline for atmosphere, and chemistry between two dance partners that was palatable. They had just finished a dance and Yaro had made no move to leave the dance floor, when the piano player asked for everyone's attention. "Ladies and gentlemen, it is my pleasure to introduce to you the future Mr. and Mrs. Yaro Bomou." Immediately, cheers and clapping hands signaled the room's congratulations. Leisa was speechless. As she stared at Yaro in amazement, he said, "Will you marry me?"

"Oh God, yes. Yes!" Leisa was in tears. "And thank you for such a romantic way of asking me. She closed her eyes as he moved to kiss her amid more cheers. It was not one of his passionate, I-am-going-to-ravish-you-now kisses, but the fact that he kissed her there on the dance floor was incredible.

Leisa chose the darkness of the cab to speak of the remaining culturally unacceptable aspect of their relationship. "Yaro, you do realize that I am twelve years older than you, and not now of course, but one day that could be a burden to you."

Slowly and deliberately he replied, "Ah, for sure. You will grow older. And what would you have me do with that fact, Diarabi? More importantly, what kind of thoughts do you have about it?

Damn, thought Leisa, he catches on fast.

Since she didn't answer, he continued. "Do you feel like a victim of your age? Do you want me to be concerned about some possible future disability in you? Or is it a matter of what society thinks? The man must be older than the woman? Which of these thoughts, is creating your reality of caution – or is it all of them?"

What have I done to be so rewarded, thought Leisa, as she tried to stop her tears and fashion an appropriate response. To have such a man in her life! To finally have not one single doubt about being in love with him forever.

There was no need to answer his questions. Instead, she said, as she turned to him and placed her hands on his face, "My own destined love, no more taboos!"